The

HANDBOOK

of

JUMPING

ESSENTIALS

Also by
François
Lemaire de Ruffieu

The Handbook of Riding Essentials

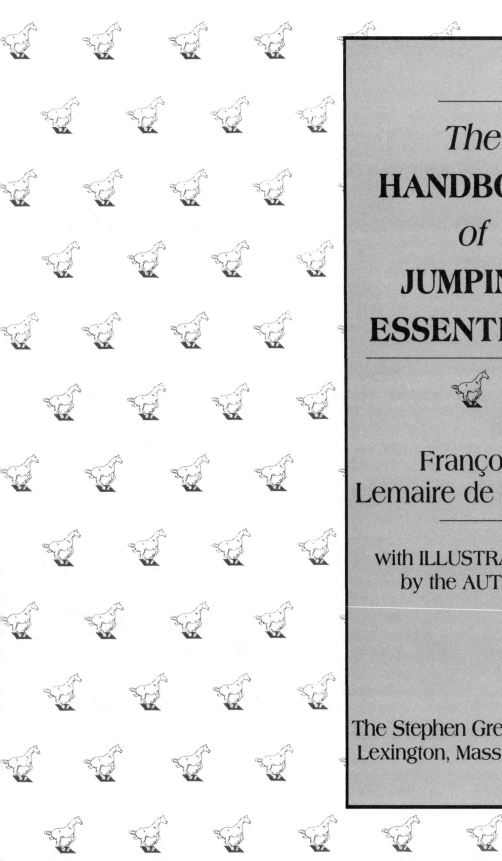

The
HANDBOOK
of
JUMPING
ESSENTIALS

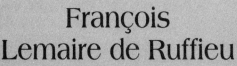

François Lemaire de Ruffieu

with ILLUSTRATIONS
by the AUTHOR

The Stephen Greene Press
Lexington, Massachusetts

THE STEPHEN GREENE PRESS, INC.
Published by the Penguin Group
Viking Penguin Inc., 40 West 23rd Street, New York, New York 10010, U.S.A.
Penguin Books Ltd, 27 Wrights Lane, London W8 5TZ, England
Penguin Books Australia Ltd, Ringwood, Victoria, Australia
Penguin Books Canada Ltd, 2801 John Street, Markham, Ontario, Canada L3R 1B4
Penguin Books (N.Z.) Ltd, 182-190 Wairau Road, Auckland 10, New Zealand

Penguin Books Ltd, Registered Offices: Harmondsworth, Middlesex, England

First published in 1988 by The Stephen Greene Press, Inc.
Published simultaneously in Canada
Distributed by Viking Penguin Inc.

Grateful acknowledgment is made for permission to use the following material:

Registered trademarks of The Coca-Cola Company, Atlanta, Georgia and PADD, Inc., Glouces-
ter, Virginia.

Five rein effects and illustrations from *The Handbook of Riding Essentials* by François Lemaire
de Ruffieu. Copyright © 1986 by François Lemaire de Ruffieu. Reprinted by permission of
Harper & Row, Publishers, Inc.

Illustrations by the author
Designed by Deborah Schneider
Produced by Unicorn Production Services, Inc.
Printed in the United States of America
by Haddon Craftsmen
Set in Americana and Caslon #540

Library of Congress Cataloging-in-Publication Data
Lemaire de Ruffieu, François.
   The handbook of jumping essentials.
   1. Jumping (Horsemanship) I. Title.
SF309.7.L38 1988   798.2′5   88-1170
ISBN 0-8289-0679-3

This book is dedicated to the memory of Maître Jean Couillaud, who was a beloved teacher. An exceptional personage and a true horseman, he was indeed, and his students do not have to close their eyes to still see him, hear him, and benefit from his immeasurable knowledge of horsemanship.

This book is also dedicated to my uncle, the Colonel Jean Gailly de Taurines, who in the 1930s, was one of the best riders representing France in the international show jumping competitions.

I would also like to express much appreciation to Beverly Pellegrini, without whose efforts this book would not have been realized.

Preface • xi
Introduction • xiii

**One
The Spot**

What Is the Spot?   1
Where Is the Spot Located?   1
How Does the Horse Jump from the Spot?   2
How Big Is the Spot?   5
How Does the Rider Bring the Horse to the Spot   6
  Box?
How Does the Rider See and Adjust a Distance?   7
  Part 1: Learning to See a Distance   7
  Part 2: Learning to Feel the Takeoff   14
  Part 3: Bringing the Horse to the Right Spot   19
  Part 4: The Spots within a Line of Obstacles   22

**Two
The Education
of the Rider**

The Rider's Position   28
Over the Fences — Forward Position   29
On the Flat "in Suspension" Half Seat   30
Exercises for the Rider   33
  The Forward Position   33
  Lower Body Exercises   35
  Upper Body Exercises   35
  Part 1: Learning to Maintain the Forward Position   37
  Part 2: Learning to Develop Strength and Good   40
    Timing in Your Lower Legs
  Part 3: Learning to Develop the Timing of Your   42
    Upper Body
  Part 4: Learning to Hold the Forward Position   45
    between Two Obstacles

Part 5: Learning to Switch from a Forward Position   48
    to a Half Seat
Part 6: Learning to Switch from a Forward to a   51
    Sitting Position
Part 7: Learning to Approach a Single Obstacle   53
    at the Canter
Part 8: Learning to Approach an In-and-Out   56
    Combination
Part 9: Learning to Turn before, on Top of, and   58
    after the Obstacle
Part 10: Learning to Jump a Course   61
    Learning the Course   61
    The Warm-up   62

**Three
The Education
of the Horse**

How Much Should Your Horse Know?   67
Learning to Start a Horse over Fences   68
Jumping on the Longe Line at Semiliberty over a   68
Single Obstacle
Jumping on the Longe Line over an In-and-Out   72
Combination
Jumping under Saddle   77
    Teaching the Horse to Jump a Single Obstacle at   78
    the Trot
    Teaching the Horse to Jump Several Obstacles   80
    at the Trot
    Teaching the Horse to Jump a Single Obstacle   82
    at the Canter
    Hints on How to Improve Your Horse's Style over   86
    Fences
    Teaching the Horse to Lengthen and to Shorten   88
    His Strides to Meet a Spot
    Teaching the Horse to Jump a Double and a   92
    Triple Combination

Teaching the Horse to Turn on Top of an Obstacle   97

  Preparation on the Flat   97
  Bending Lines   98
  The Turns   100
Teaching Your Horse to Jump Courses   102
Jumping a Low Course at the Trot   102
Jumping a Low Course at the Canter   103
General Ideas about Various Types of Courses   104
Hunter Courses   104
Equitation Courses   105
Jumper Courses   106
Teaching and Improving the Horse's Flat Work   110
Flat Work on the Longe Line   111
Gaits and Transitions   112
The Lengthening and the Shortening of the Strides   114
The Lateral Movements   114
The Counter Canter and the Flying Change of Lead   114
The Half-Halt   115

Concluding Remarks   117
Appendix: The Five Rein Effects   119
About the Author   123

Before you begin to work over fences, remember for your safety that it is always to your best advantage to wear gear and clothes especially designed for the sport you have chosen. Tack shops are well supplied with all kinds of equipment you may need when riding horses.

Please *do not* attempt any kind of jumping before making certain that:

THE RIDER: has a well-fitted helmet with a chin strap; wears riding boots or paddock boots.

Also, make sure that a rider ties long hair to stay away from the face so that it will not cause momentary blindness. All clothes must be buttoned and tucked in. The shoes must not have flat soles (such as sneakers) that could easily slip forward or backward in the stirrup irons.

THE HORSE: The bit must be well fitted and the bridle properly adjusted. The girth must *always* be tightened one more time before beginning to jump. The horse must wear galloping boots to protect his tendons. The horse must wear bell boots to protect his heels.

It is important that all leather be supple, well oiled, and in good condition to avoid breaking when riding.

THE OBSTACLES: No unused cups should remain on the standards. The rails and the wings must be in good shape without splinters or protruding nails.

The footing around the obstacles must be flat and free of rocks, branches, any awkward items, etc.

Never forget that a rider, any rider, must not jump a horse without having someone knowledgeable watching.

Remember that jumping is a very tiring exercise for the horse, so do not abuse his willingness. A few jumps per session will be enough. Also, do not omit considering his general health and soundness, and check to make certain his shoes are tightly fitted on his hooves.

"*Oh, no!* She missed her spot!" thought Dawn, standing near the in-gate at the Tulsa Horse Show grounds.

As a trainer, she was attentively watching one of her students jumping an equitation course. The round completed, the rider stepped out of the arena with the most unusual nervousness. She was very upset. . . .

"Come here, young lady," called Dawn out loud when she saw her prize student walking away.

At these words, the rider stopped, turned around, and began complaining frantically, "I need to buy glasses with wipers on or maybe sell peanuts at the coliseum, but certainly not ride horses, besides . . ."

"Hold it, hold it right there!" interrupted Dawn with authority.

"Do you believe it? I—gave—the—class—away!" continued the rider, not daring to look at her trainer as tears began to well in her eyes.

"Come on, will you—take two deep breaths and calm down," suggested Dawn, speaking now with a softer tone of voice.

"_____"

"Good. Now explain to me what really happened," requested Dawn as she was, by force of habit, correcting the position of the rider's stirrup iron.

"I wanted . . . I was . . ." mumbled the rider, but suddenly able to verbalize her thoughts, she added, speaking very quickly, "Everything was going according to plan until I was in line with this dumb coop. Then I went blank! Zip, nothing, zero! I COULD NOT SEE MY SPOT! ANY SPOT! So I froze, and my horse took the jump too soon. Didn't you see?"

"Of course, I saw it," replied Dawn with great calm. Then smiling, she added, "I have to admit that your jump made the Golden Gate Bridge look like a miniature. . . . Anyway, even though you forgot what to do in a case like that, you still looked fine over the fence. You can believe that."

"Hmmm . . . really?" asked the rider with brighter eyes and showing the beginning of a timid smile.

"You know," added Dawn, "the way you feel and the way you

look are often two different things. . . ."

The trainer was right. Ten minutes later when the horse show announcer called for the results, the rider, who only moments ago was filled with despair, won a red ribbon.

This horse show scene sounds very familiar, does it not?

All over the country, or should I say, all over the world, when it comes to jumping, trainers and riders, at any level, are concerned about the same subject: the take-off spot.

But what is it? Where is it? How does one learn about it?

Fascinated by the questions, I began searching for more precise answers. Fortunate enough to travel to several countries, I was able to accumulate information and reduce this big problem to workable little solutions.

At the insistence of my students, who always want to know everything, and for all the riders I have yet to meet, I have tried to become a writer again and condense into print the fruit of my research. I also have sharpened my pencils to practice my drawing skills, thinking that the handmade pictures will better aid your understanding.

The following pages are of main interest to broaden the rider's knowledge and to develop a true *self-confidence*. Yes, many riders are afraid . . . of course, not afraid to jump, but of feeling inadequate to *see a spot*. As a result, many consistently hold an apprehension in their minds and may jeopardize the actions of their horses. Contrary to the common belief, a rider, any rider, does not need a natural talent to evaluate a distance. All that is required is a real desire to study, not to underestimate one's own capabilities, and to follow a proven system.

In this book, I simplified and reorganized essential basics of which any rider should be aware. In Chapter I, I explain what the spot is and how one could define its location. I also propose a simple method to accustom the rider's eyes to see a distance, and also how to bring the horse within this spot area. Chapter II gives an exposé of the rider's position over fences and several exercises to perfect this position while jumping a course. In Chapter III, I explain one of the ways to teach or to re-school a horse to jump with ease and proper form, and to learn to find the most comfortable takeoff spot.

To be successful, these pages should be followed step-by-step, going from one exercise to the next. The key to success is constant repetition and patience. Remember the old adage: "He who goes slowly progresses rapidly."

In other words, what is properly assimilated does not have to be re-learned again. But too many riders are very impatient and want everything . . . yesterday. Sorry! It does not work like this with horses. It is, indeed, a slow process, but with proper time invested, the rewards will be endless.

—François

Postscript

To specify a leg or hand action in the pages that follow, I will use the words act, resist, and yield; also, from time to time, I will refer to a numbered rein effect (I, II, III, etc.). All of these expressions have already been clearly explained in my preceding work, *The Handbook of Riding Essentials*. A summary appears in the appendix at the end of this book.

The
HANDBOOK
of
JUMPING
ESSENTIALS

One

The
SPOT

In jumping, the spot is the common name given to the most suitable place from which a horse should leave the ground to clear an obstacle with ease and minimum effort.

WHERE IS the SPOT LOCATED?

The spot is always located in front of every obstacle at a specific distance that is determined by the height of the jump. For example, the spot for a 3 foot 6 inch (1.05 m) obstacle, on average, will be approximately 4 feet (1.2 m) in front of it. But the exact position of the spot can vary and changes with the type of obstacle to be jumped.

There are basically two different shapes of obstacles:

- Narrow, called upright fences or verticals. (See Fig. 1A.)
- Wide, called spread fences or oxers. (See Fig. 1B.)

All of the other kinds, such as chicken coops, walls, liverpools, triple bars, etc., are only variations or combinations of these two types.

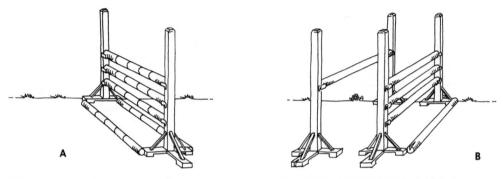

FIG. 1

A rail is a wooden pole and must be about 14 feet long and 4 inches in diameter. For a narrow obstacle, the rails should not be shorter than 6 feet.

IMPORTANT

As a general rule, to accomplish an equal arc over two different types of obstacles of the same height, the horse should take off from a normal, average spot for a vertical fence (see Fig. 2A) and from a closer spot for a spread (see Fig. 2B).

HOW DOES the HORSE JUMP from the SPOT?

During the approach to a 3½-foot vertical obstacle, a trained horse cantering on the right lead (for instance) will be balanced, steady in his rhythm, and attentive to the rider's natural aids. At about 6 feet (1.8 m) away from the obstacle, he should be on his left diagonal biped, i.e., the second beat of the canter. (See Fig. 3.)

The HANDBOOK of JUMPING ESSENTIALS

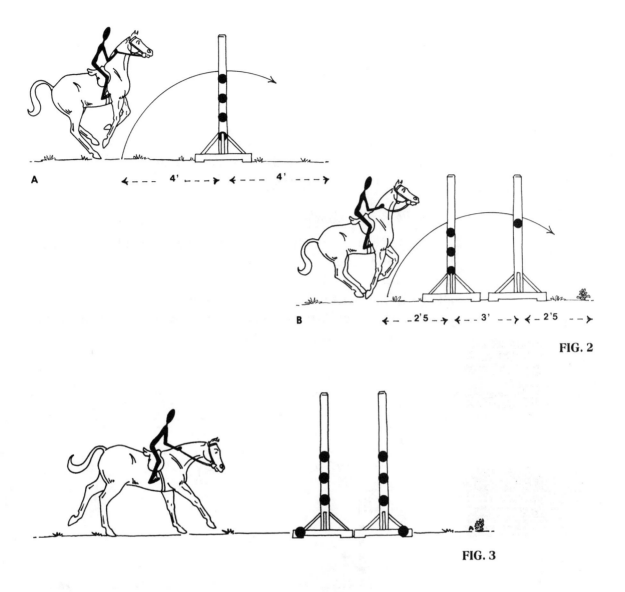

A

B

FIG. 2

FIG. 3

1st Phase: The takeoff.

The horse will lengthen his neck, lower his head, and reach the ground with his right foreleg (the lead) at about 2 feet ahead of the left foreleg. To balance himself, he will shorten his neck, raise his head, and then, about 4 feet (1.2 m) from the obstacle, lift his forehand, folding his forelegs. With an adequate thrust from his bent hocks and hind legs, he will propel himself into the air. (See Fig. 4A.)

Note: to jump an obstacle over 4 feet in height, the horse will no longer lower his head and neck, but collect himself.

2nd Phase: The suspension time.

On top of the fence (i.e., when he is in the air), he will stretch and lower his neck to free his shoulders and round his spinal column from the ears to the tail. All four legs will be tucked up, close to his body. (See Fig. 4B.)

3rd Phase: The landing.

The horse will stretch his forelegs, raise his head to rebalance himself, and reach for the ground with his feet. He will land about 4 feet after the obstacle. Then he will lower his neck to allow his hind legs to better come under his body and to sustain a round top line. After landing, the horse will most likely be on the left lead canter. (See Fig. 4C.)

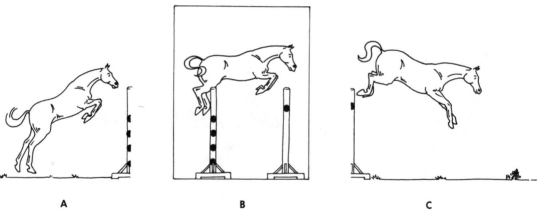

A　　　　　　　　B　　　　　　　　C

FIG. 4

IMPORTANT

The rider must also realize that when the horse takes off to jump, he always leaves the ground in two distinct movements:

1ST MOVEMENT: the forelegs leave the ground at the same time.

2ND MOVEMENT: then the hind legs leave the ground. Most of the time, the hind legs leave the ground almost from the same place as the forelegs, but sometimes they will move more forward, closer to the obstacle.

A horse will rarely leave the ground from the exact same place every time. For a 3 foot 6 inch vertical fence, he may take off anywhere between 4 feet to 6 feet (1.2 m–1.8 m) in front of the obstacle. So the spot area will have about 2 feet (60 cm) in depth and also be as wide as the horse's body. We could conclude that for a 3 foot 6 inch obstacle, the spot area looks like an imaginary 2-foot-square box, 4 feet from the obstacle and directly in line with its center. (See Fig. 5.)

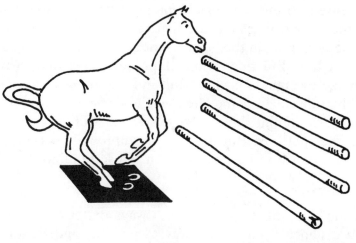

FIG. 5

To attempt a jump, the horse has to have his two forelegs on the ground at the same time. The only moment this will occur is just after the second phase of the canter (i.e., the diagonal biped is on the ground) when the leading foreleg reaches the ground. (See Fig. 3.)

Knowing this, the rider, when necessary, will have to adjust the horse's stride in such a manner that the two forelegs will be within the imaginary *spot box* area before taking off.

HOW DOES the RIDER BRING the HORSE to the SPOT BOX?

An "educated" rider will approach an obstacle, checking to do the following:

- Maintain the horse's balance.
- Control the pace (rhythm).
- Sustain the impulsion (the desire to move forward).
- Adjust the horse's stride.

If these determining factors are correctly established, the horse will jump with ease. But if one is missing, the horse may take off from either too far or too close to the obstacle. In either case, the rider will have to make a snap decision to properly correct the stride to bring the horse's foreleg within the spot box.

If the rider realizes too late that the horse will jump from too far, a lengthening in the horse's stride will be necessary to reach the spot box. But this action, improperly executed, may shift the horse's weight to his forehand and risk knocking a rail down.

If the rider realizes too late that the horse will jump from too close, a shortening in the horse's stride will be necessary to reach the spot box. But this action, improperly executed, may incite the horse to hesitate or even refuse to jump.

IMPORTANT

While jumping a course, it is always better for the rider to see a distance from as far away as possible and to adjust the horse's stride very discreetly.

For this question, considering that several factors are involved, I will answer in four distinct parts. In the first part, you will learn how to see a distance; in the second part, you will learn to feel the take-off phase of the jumping; in the third part,

you will learn how to bring the horse to the spot box; and in the fourth part, you will learn about spot boxes within a combination of two fences.

Part 1: Learning to See a Distance

A. You must begin by developing your sense of feel. What you need is to realize, while cantering, when your horse has his leading foreleg on the ground.

You probably have already learned that at the canter the horse makes three successive beats followed by a phase of suspension with his four legs off the ground. Let us briefly review this gait for the right lead canter (see Fig. 6— it will be opposite for the left lead):

1ST BEAT: the horse engages his left hind leg forward under his body.

2ND BEAT: the horse propels his left diagonal biped forward; i.e., the left foreleg and the right hind leg, simultaneously.

3RD BEAT: the horse thrusts his right foreleg forward (the lead); then the horse has a suspension phase before beginning again with the first beat.

1st beat   2nd beat   3rd beat   suspension

FIG. 6

At the beginning, while cantering, you may seek the assistance of a Gentil Helper, who is going to point out to you every time your horse touches the ground with his leading foreleg. Very soon you will realize that before it occurs, your horse will slightly lower his head and neck.

HELPFUL SUGGESTION

The average length of a stride is about 9 to 12 feet (2.7 m–3.6 m), so that when cantering the horse will reach the ground with his leading foreleg every 9 to 12 feet.

B. As soon as you are able to very distinctly realize when your horse is at the third beat of the canter, with your eyes open at first and then closed to better feel the motion, ride a few strides and, in rhythm, *count out loud* the third beat about ten times in a row.

Then canter all the way around the riding ring, still counting out loud (no whispering) a series of ten even beats as many times as you are able. (See Fig. 7.)

FIG. 7

This simple exercise will quickly develop your sense of feel and amazingly, as you practice more, will also teach you:

- To control your breathing.
- To establish a quiet rhythm at the canter.
- To maintain your horse's balance.

The HANDBOOK of JUMPING ESSENTIALS

These components are essential to jump a course of several fences.

C. Now ask your Gentil Helper to trace with his or her foot, two long parallel lines perpendicular to the track at about 2 feet (60 cm) apart. (See Fig. 8.) If the horse is easily impressionable by new things, such as recent markings on the ground, it is advisable to allow him to walk once or twice over these lines. Then, cantering toward them, try to guess the stride that will put your horse's leading foreleg within the 2 feet enclosed by these lines. Do not be afraid to be wrong! It may take you a few trials before you are able to guess correctly every time. Practice and routine will improve your judgment.

FIG. 8

You may also ask your Gentil Helper to draw several sets of parallel lines at least 100 feet (30 m) apart around the ring. The more you drill, the faster you will learn.

D. When you are able to clearly see this final stride without hesitation, try to find the two last strides before the parallel lines. Then try three and, progressively, increase to six and even eight or more. After practicing this exercise daily for a week or two, you unconsciously will be able to recognize how six, seven, or eight strides look. Then, automatically, you will determine, with accuracy, with which of these distances you will feel most comfortable. (See Fig. 9.)

Remember: the farther you are capable of seeing a distance, the easier it will be to effect, when necessary, the appropriate adjustment to the horse's stride.

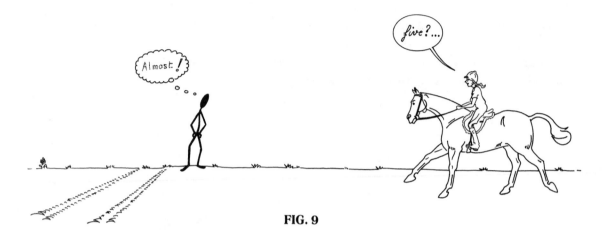

FIG. 9

E. At this point, you will realize that sometimes your horse's leading foreleg reaches the ground either near the front parallel line or closer to the back one.

YOU MUST AIM FOR THE MIDPOINT IN BETWEEN THESE TWO LINES.

So, if you feel that your last stride will not quite reach this midpoint, you will have to make an adjustment in your striding and ask your horse to lengthen the canter. (See Fig. 10.) To do so:

SEAT: in light contact with the saddle with your upper body slightly tilted forward.

LEGS: acting together at the girth, but preferably just below your knees (softer action) to avoid rushing the gait.

HANDS: softly yielding to release the contact with the horse's mouth without disturbing his balance.

FIG. 10 Lengthen the stride

F. If you feel that your last stride will fall too far after this midpoint, you will have to execute an adjustment to your striding and ask your horse to shorten the canter. (See Fig. 11.) To do so:

FIG. 11 Shorten the stride

SEAT: deeper into the saddle with your upper body erect to encourage the horse to slow the pace.

LEGS: resist together at the girth to sustain the engagement of the horse's hind legs.

HANDS: act together by squeezing your fingers on the reins; and if it is not enough, apply a series of discreet half-halts (see Chapter Three, page 115).

G. Try to approach the lines from a left-hand turn and then from a right turn. To adjust the distance, you simply have to shorten the curve if you are too far and widen it if you need more space.

SEAT: light in the saddle with more weight on your inside stirrup iron.

LEGS: the inside leg resists at the girth to maintain the impulsion and the bending of the horse's spinal column. The outside leg resists behind the girth to forbid the eventual drifting of the haunches to the outside.

HANDS: the inside hand acts as a leading rein (see appendix, Rein Effect I) to encourage the horse to look where he is going. The outside hand yields to allow and then to regulate the action of the inside rein.

To facilitate the turn and to make the distance work, constantly focus on the middle between these lines and slightly rotate your waist in such a way that your outside shoulder points in the direction you wish to follow; i.e., for a left turn your right shoulder will be pointing forward and almost to the left. (See Fig. 12.) This action will also trigger the release of the outside rein and indicate to the horse when to turn.

H. Ask your Gentil Helper to design a fictitious course of several sets of parallel lines and play cantering this pattern, adjusting the strides as you go along. To better check how well you are doing and to see where the horse has stepped, it will be a very good idea to rake the ground around and in between these two lines.

Remember at this point: if you encounter difficulties practicing one exercise, do not hesitate to step back in your progression

FIG. 12

and review the preceding ones. Avoid attempting the next part until you can smoothly ride the one you are working on.

HELPFUL SUGGESTION

To train your eyes to visualize a distance, you do not have to always be riding a horse. You can easily practice on the street, at home, where you study, at work, etc. For example, wherever you are, stop for a second, look around, pick a place far enough from where you stand, such as a tree, a building corner, a door entrance, etc., and estimate how many of your own steps you need to reach it. Then pace off this distance and determine if you were correct. Time and practice will give you the accuracy you seek.

I. Practice now on a similar course, but this time add standards or wings. Make sure that they are placed about 3 feet (90 cm) beyond the farthest parallel lines. IMPORTANT: When you ride the course, do not let the wings distract you. Instead, discipline yourself to focus on the parallel lines area. (See Fig. 13, next page.)

J. Add a rail between each standard and ride the same course several times. Constant practice will develop your awareness to see a distance as well as your sense of feeling.

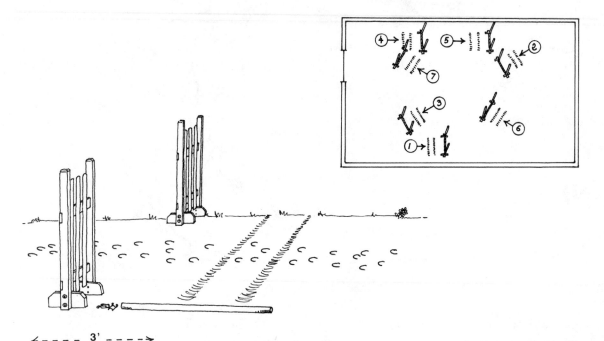

FIG. 13

When you have become familiar with this exercise, ask your Gentil Helper to draw spot boxes on the ground, instead of parallel lines, and continue practicing to bring the horse's forelegs within this space.

Part 2: Learning to Feel the Takeoff

A. With your Gentil Helper, set up an "in-and-out" combination (two obstacles in a row, separated by at least 18 feet or 5.4 m) on the track. To build these fences you will need two sets of two standards and also two sets of three rails. Place the first obstacle 50 feet (15 m) from the beginning of the long side of the ring and the second at about 18 feet beyond this point.

Between each set of standards, pile three rails in a pyramid shape. About 40 feet (12 m) before the first obstacle, place two markers, such as plastic cones, on either side of the track at least 20 feet (6 m) apart. (See Fig. 14.)

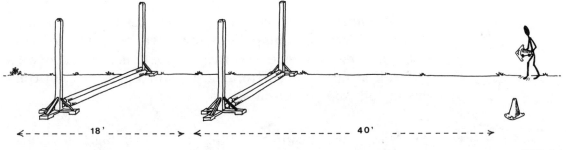

<--------- 18' ---------> <------------------ 40' ---------->

FIG. 14

B. To be certain that your horse will work calmly, walk back and forth several times through the combination. Then do the same at the posting and sitting trot. Keep on going over this line of fences until your horse is completely quiet and relaxed and does not try to jump the piles of rails. (See Fig. 15.)

FIG. 15

C. Build an 18-inch (45-cm) cross with the rails of the second fence. Make sure that one of the three rails remains lying on the ground in front of it.

Trot over the line several times, always beginning with the fence that has the rails still on the ground, and release your rein contact to allow the horse to jump by himself. It would be wise at this point to always ask him to come back to a standstill a few strides after the jump. This action will teach your horse to rebalance himself following the fence. It may be somewhat difficult at first, but before long, he will anticipate your command and stop almost on his own.

D. Now it will be time to build an 18-inch-high crossrail in between the first set of standards.

Far away from the combination, post to the trot and ride toward the line of obstacles. When you pass between the cones, sit to the trot and shift your weight down to your lower legs. In this manner, you will *look* as if you were sitting down and slightly leaning forward, but in fact, your weight will be in your heels and not on the seat of the saddle. Trot the first crossrail and then allow your horse to canter one stride before jumping the second fence. Leave him alone in between the combination. If your horse has the tendency to precipitate his strides before the first obstacle, lay one rail on the ground at about 9 feet (2.7 m) before the first fence. If it is not sufficient, add one, two, or three other rails, but this time at only 4 ½ feet (1.35 m) apart. These rails will arouse his attention, and eventually, he will forget to rush. (See Fig. 16.)

E. Modify the second element of the in-and-out to a low vertical fence about 2 feet (60 cm) in height. Jump this combination several times and progressively raise the top rail 3 inches by 3 inches until it is at about 3 feet (90 cm) to 3 feet and 6 inches (1.5 m). It would be a good idea at this point to ask your Gentil Helper to rake the ground in front of the second obstacle after every time you jump over the line. This will clearly show you from what spot your horse takes off to jump. (See Fig. 17.)

FIG. 16

In this type of work, the crossrail will predispose your horse to set himself to canter the second fence from the best possible spot. Your only role, for now, will be to concentrate on how it *feels* when your horse is about to take off to jump the vertical.

FIG. 17

F. Move the vertical fence back about 12 feet (3.6 m), to spread the in-and-out line and to allow your horse to canter two strides in between the obstacles. A horse's stride, cantering at an average pace (350 to 400 meters per minute; see page 108, "Study the horse's pace"), will cover an average of 12 feet of ground. So if you wish to add strides in between an 18-foot combination, you will use a multiple of 12 (see Fig. 18):

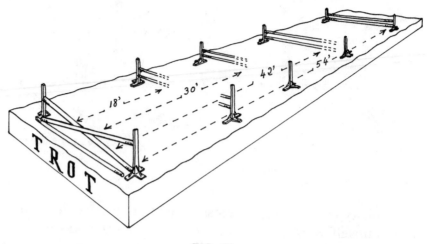

FIG. 18

- 1st stride = 18 to 21 feet (5.5 m) because it is jumped from a trot.
- 2nd stride = 18 + 12 = 30 feet (9 m).
- 3rd stride = 30 + 12 = 42 feet (12.8 m).
- 4th stride = 42 + 12 = 54 feet (16.4 m), etc.

The first distance is calculated to be 18 feet because this includes the landing phase of the trotting fence (about 4 feet), one short canter stride (10 feet), and the takeoff for the second element (4 feet).

G. Now the progression is very simple: if your horse has well accomplished the two-stride combination, you may, as you wish, spread the line and add a third stride, a fourth one, and so on. But remember, you will modify the distance only if your horse is jumping quietly. Also, do not forget to rake the ground to observe the footprints. This type of work will affirm your newly developed sense of feeling for the takeoff phase of the jumping after having cantered several strides. This work also will prepare you to correctly approach a single obstacle without the help of a predetermined distance.

Part 3: Bringing the Horse to the Right Spot

At the end of Part 1 of this progression, you learned how to bring the horse's forelegs into the spot box, and in Part 2, you learned to feel the takeoff phase when the horse is jumping. Now in this third part, you will be able to join these two components and learn to bring your horse to the spot box to jump a single fence. In jumping, the best way to learn to adjust the horse's stride at the canter is to begin with a single obstacle.

A. Build a crossrail fence of about 2 feet (45 cm) in height on the track. Ask your Gentil Helper to rake in front of the ground pole and trace a spot box about 18 inches before this new obstacle.

On a circle, far enough away from the crossrail, pick up the canter. Establish your pace, the horse's balance, and ride toward the fence. Look for the spot box, promptly deciding whether or not you have to execute an adjustment and act accordingly; then look up beyond the jump. DO NOT BE AFRAID TO BE WRONG IN YOUR JUDGMENT. Only people who do not do anything never make mistakes. Remember that practice will improve your decisions.

Throughout the last strides preceding the obstacle, you must use your natural aids:

SEAT: in light contact with the saddle and balanced above your feet with your upper body leaning slightly forward.

LEGS: acting together at the girth to perfect the engagement and to maintain the pace and the impulsion.

HANDS: in soft contact with the horse's mouth; always attentive to any sudden changes in the horse's balance.

B. Modify the crossrail to a low vertical fence of about 2 feet (60 cm) in height and repeat the exercise.

HELPFUL SUGGESTIONS

When you think you see a good takeoff spot, you had best wait one more stride and confirm what you perceived; then, if necessary, make the adjustment before looking up.

If you do not see your spot, wait one or two strides and look again. If you still do not discern anything and realize that you are getting closer to the obstacle, do not worry, but concentrate on the impulsion and the horse's balance to allow him to resolve the situation. It is, after all, a partnership, is it not?

C. Progressively raise the top rail 3 inches by 3 inches until you reach the height of 3 feet to 3 feet 6 inches (90 cm–1.5 m) Also, ask your Gentil Helper to move the spot box as the jump gets higher, i.e., for a 3-foot jump, the box should be 3 feet and 6 inches in front of the obstacle. (For a 3 foot 6 inch jump, it will be 4 feet, etc.) (See Fig. 19.)

Practice this exercise until you are able to bring your horse properly to the spot box every time.

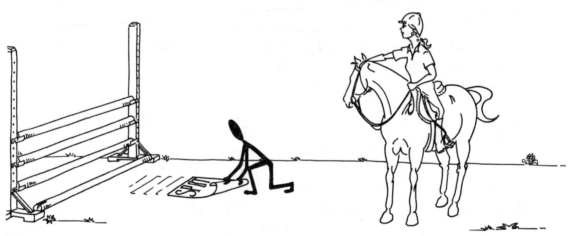

FIG. 19

D. Now, without changing the spot box, ask your Gentil Helper to build a ramped oxer type of fence approximately 3 feet in height and 2 feet (60 cm) in width. The position of the previous vertical will be used as a center for the new spread. Make sure that the first top rail is 3 inches (7.5 cm) lower than the back one. (See Fig. 20.)

The HANDBOOK of JUMPING ESSENTIALS

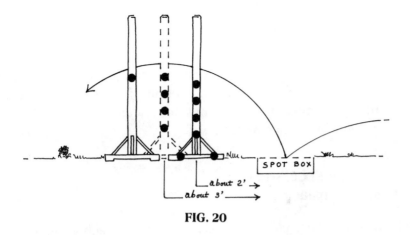

FIG. 20

To better jump the oxer, your horse will approach nearer the base, and that is why the spot box will seem closer. After you have adjusted the stride, look up; but this time, focus on the *middle of the back top rail.*

E. Progressively square the oxer until the two top rails are equal in height. Then, day after day, you may gradually widen the fence as much as your brave heart desires (see Fig. 21).

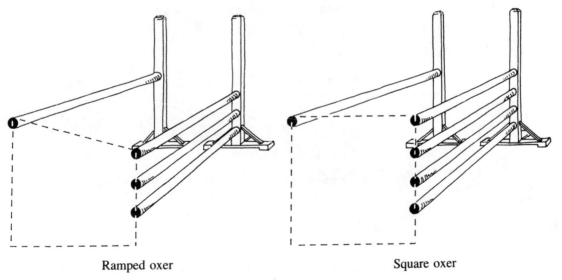

Ramped oxer   Square oxer

FIG. 21

The SPOT   21

HELPFUL SUGGESTION

When approaching a spread type of fence, you should slightly loosen the reins to allow the horse to come closer to the base and to have more freedom in the action of his forehand. Also, remember that the higher the obstacle becomes, the more effectively you must act with your legs.

Part 4: The Spots within a Line of Obstacles

In this last part, you will study how to approach a line of two fences at the canter. As you become more familiar with the spot box, the obstacles will diversify and the number of strides in between will diminish to progressively increase the difficulties.

The distance between two obstacles jumped at the canter may vary in relation to their height and also to the horse's speed. But for a one-stride in-and-out with obstacles at about 3 feet 6 inches (1.5 m) in height, the average measurement is approximately 24 feet to 26 feet (7.2 m–7.8 m). This, of course, includes the landing after the first element (6 feet or 1.8 m), one canter stride (12 feet or 3.6 m), and the takeoff of the second fence (6 feet or 1.8 m). (See Fig. 22.) You may conclude that for a combination of two fences:

- One stride: 6 + 12 + 6 = 24 feet (7.2 m).
- Two strides: 24 + 12 = 36 feet (10.8 m).
- Three strides: 36 + 12 = 48 feet (14.4 m), etc.

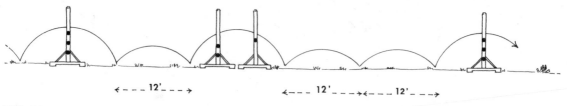

FIG. 22

To spread or to reduce a line, adding or subtracting strides, you will calculate using multiples of 12.

The HANDBOOK of JUMPING ESSENTIALS

A. With your Gentil Helper, build a line of two vertical obstacles, with six strides in between (about 84 feet or 25.2 m). Rake and trace the spot boxes. Even though you may not need it as much, let us not be hasty in our progression.

Then, away from this line, pick up the canter, and when you have organized the basic components for balance, rhythm, and impulsion, go toward the fences. *Remember:* YOU MUST FIND THE SPOT TO MAKE A CORRECTION. If, for your first trial, you do not see anything, or if you are not too sure whether to lengthen or shorten the stride, DO NEITHER; instead, concentrate on your horse's balance, rhythm, and impulsion.

If you jump over the first obstacle, missing your spot and taking off either too soon or too late, you will have enough space to execute a discreet adjustment on the other side to properly meet the second spot area.

If you land *too close* to the first element, you will have to move up to recover the missing distance. Your actions should be:

SEAT: lean forward to compel the increase of pace.

LEGS: act stronger at the girth, but NOT faster, to avoid rushing the horse's gait.

HANDS: slightly yield, but still control the horse's balance.

If you land *too far* from the first element, you will have to shorten the horse's stride to re-establish the correct distance. Your actions should be:

SEAT: sit deeper in the saddle with your upper body erect to incite the horse to slow.

LEGS: in contact with the horse's barrel to preserve the engagement and the impulsion.

HANDS: resist and, if necessary, apply discreet half-halts (see Chapter Three, page 115) to shorten the stride.

Note: were you aware that the best riders are always adjusting their strides? You may not see it because they have learned to act with smoothness and discretion in using their natural aids.

B. As you jump the line, successively transform the second and then the first obstacle to an oxer type. Your ride will be similar, providing that the center of the new spread corresponds to the exact placement of the preceding vertical.

HELPFUL SUGGESTIONS

For a line with two obstacles set at a normal distance, you may slightly increase the horse's pace to jump a vertical followed by a spread and loosen the reins inside the combination to allow the horse to take off closer to the second element (see Fig. 23).

FIG. 23

To jump first a spread and then a vertical, you will have to steady the pace to better approach the first element and readjust your reins inside the combination to incite the horse to take off from a longer spot (see Fig. 24).

FIG. 24

The HANDBOOK of JUMPING ESSENTIALS

To jump a spread followed by a spread, you will have to steady the pace and loosen your reins to better approach the first element and repeat the same for the second.

When jumping a vertical to a vertical, to better approach and meet a comfortable takeoff spot for the first element, you will have to maintain the horse's pace and keep the reins adjusted. In between the combination, you will have to repeat the same leg and hand actions to obtain a similar takeoff spot.

C. Seeking a spot from a turn is basically the same idea. The difference is that you must be able to change direction with ease using your natural aids with the greatest discretion. To accomplish a comfortable turn, you must sustain your horse's balance, look where you wish to go, and act with your:

SEAT: shifting your weight in the direction you want to go.

LEGS: the inside leg acting at the girth to preserve the impulsion; the outside leg resisting behind the girth to forbid the haunches from drifting away.

HANDS: maintaining an equal contact with the horse's mouth and then slightly releasing the outside rein to allow the turn.

If you see a long spot, DO NOT SUCCUMB to the temptation to run for it, but rather wait for a better distance.

If you feel that the spot is too close, you may shorten the turn to reduce the number of strides to find a more suitable spot.

If you feel that the spot is too far away, you may widen the turn to add strides to find a better spot.

If you do not like the distance and cannot decide, allow your horse to find a spot on his own but MAINTAIN the balance, rhythm, and impulsion.

D. A course designer may want to test the riders' and the horses' adjustabilities by setting some average distances and also some short and long ones. The difference is only a matter of a few inches or a few feet, but the horse cannot realize it when he approaches the first fence. The only time the horse will be aware of it is when he is closer to the second element, but he may not be able to correct himself in time to jump safely. On the other hand, if you, the rider, know *when* the line is short or long, you may ride accordingly:

- A short line will necessitate closer spots.
- A long line will necessitate longer spots.

In your progression, practice jumping the line now several times and, from time to time, shorten or lengthen the distance.

E. Now lessen the number of strides by simply reducing the distance between the two obstacles and progressively end with a one-stride in-and-out. A 24-foot combination of two obstacles is in fact easy to jump. The only difficulty resides in the approach to the first element. But if you prepare your approach, cantering slightly more forward than you were when jumping one single fence, and if you bring your horse to the right spot, you will have no problem obtaining a smooth and easy ride. But if you miss that spot, you will be either too short or too long.

If you jump the first obstacle from too short a spot, do not lengthen the stride in between, or you will end too close to the second fence. Instead, wait. To do so:

SEAT: hold your upper body slightly erect to slow the horse.

LEGS: hold a steady pressure to preserve the engagement of the hind legs.

HANDS: resist on the reins and, if necessary, apply a discreet half-halt (see Chapter Three, page 115) to hold the strides.

If you jump the first obstacle from too long a spot, lengthen the stride in between to incite your horse to take off from a far spot again. To do so:

SEAT: slightly lean your upper body forward to increase the pace.

LEGS: act together stronger, but not *faster*, to avoid rushing your horse.

HANDS: briefly release the contact to allow the horse to stretch his neck and head and then increase the contact to cause the horse to take off sooner.

HELPFUL SUGGESTIONS

Ride a tight in-and-out:

1. As you approach the obstacle, look for a close spot that will lead you to a short landing on the other side.

2. Shorten the stride in between the fences to avoid getting too close to the second element.

Ride a wide in-and-out:

1. As you approach the obstacle, look for a long spot that will lead you to a long landing on the other side.

2. Lengthen the stride in between the fences to come closer to the second element.

In a triple combination, a one stride to a two stride or vice versa, it will be as easy, unless one of the two distances is shorter or longer than the other. In this case, to adjust, you will have to focus on the middle obstacle. (See Fig. 25.) (See page 94, the triple combination.)

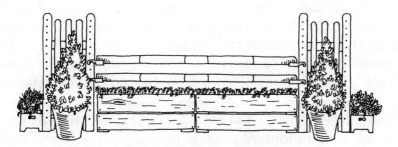

FIG. 25 Vertical obstacle with rails and brush boxes

Two

The
EDUCATION
of the
RIDER

The concept of riding with the upper body leaning forward was originated in the United States. To maintain better balance and to obtain greater speed, the American jockeys shortened their stirrup leathers and adopted a more forward position in their riding. At the beginning of the twentieth century, their incontestable success at the overseas racetrack created a big commotion in Europe. Fascinated by the novelty, the Italian riders studied the principle of balance behind this revolutionary new way to ride horses, and along with the French school, they submitted a new method to the show jumping world. The years went by, and the forward position proved itself in giving to the rider a better opportunity to jump higher, wider, and even faster.

The RIDER'S POSITION

When you maintain a forward position, you allow your horse to jump freely to the best of his abilities. *Remember:* a well-balanced weight is a weight easy to carry (see Fig. 26).

OVER the FENCES— FORWARD POSITION

• Your seat must be slightly out of the saddle, directly above your feet.

• Your upper body is tilted forward with your spinal column flat and relaxed.

• Your shoulders, equally open, are totally relaxed.

• Your head is held up, your chin pointing slightly forward and above the horse's crest (upper part of the neck).

• Your eyes, attentive, are looking forward or toward the next obstacle.

• Your arms are down and ready to move forward to release the reins in response to the horse's need to stretch.

• Your elbows, open and relaxed, are near the horse's neck.

• Your forearms are parallel and in line with the horse's crest.

• Your wrists are held in line with your forearms.

• Your hands, in line with your forearms, but slightly lower than the horse's crest, are *always above the horse's mouth.*

• Your thumbs and index fingers hold the reins firmly, the thumbnails facing up. The other fingers are relaxed.

• Your thighs are in light contact with the saddle.

• Your knees are in light contact with the saddle.

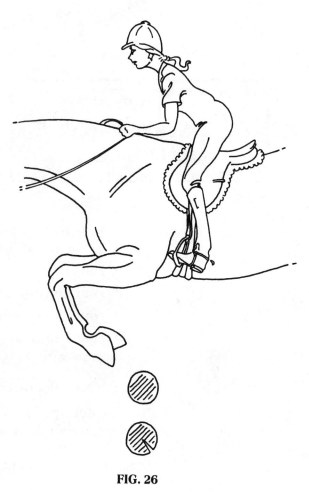

FIG. 26

- Your lower legs (calves) are in TIGHT contact with the horse's barrel; the stirrup leather should remain perpendicular to the ground.
- Your ankles, flexed, are relaxed and springy.
- Your feet, at the girth (actually 4 to 6 inches behind), tightly hold each stirrup base by the balls of your feet, with more weight on the inside of the stirrup iron. Each stirrup iron is almost perpendicular to the horse's body, the outside branch pointing slightly forward.
- Your heels are lower than your toes and carry most of your weight.
- Your toes maintain a natural angle from the horse's side (25 to 35 degrees).

On the FLAT "in SUSPENSION" HALF SEAT

This position is used while you are approaching an obstacle to jump or for speed. It is often called hunt seat, balanced seat, or 2-point position. The only differences between this and the jumping position are in the seat and the upper body:

- Your seat is almost in contact with the saddle, but most of your weight still remains in your heels.
- Your upper body is slightly leaning forward.
- Your arms drop naturally and are close to your rib cage.
- Your elbows are near your hips.
- Your hands are held 4 to 5 inches apart and level with the horse's withers.

HELPFUL SUGGESTIONS

To determine if your balance is sufficient, you should be able to maintain the forward position without holding onto the reins or constantly moving your feet. In case of a loss of equilibrium, on the flat or over fences, instead of falling backward, i.e., being left behind the motion or, as it is referred to in riding, "calling a taxi", simply educate yourself to simultaneously tighten your calves and lower your seat closer to the saddle.

Try to avoid anticipating the inclination of your upper body, or you may be preceding the horse's motion and interfere with his jumping. Instead, opt for a more passive action—follow the horse and let him give you the proper body incline.

Your shoulders, elbows, and wrists must remain relaxed to be able to release and also follow the horse's head and neck when he stretches to clear an obstacle.

During the jumping phase, your lower legs should remain *tight* to maintain a good grip on the horse's barrel. Too weak legs would make you lose your balance and in some cases cause a fall.

Your weight should remain mostly in your heels: the lower your weight is, the less you will move on your horse. Let me ask you, in comparison, what is more difficult to move? A single standard base down or up? (See Fig. 27.)

FIG. 27

To secure the balance, it is not uncommon for a rider to discreetly position one leg slightly more forward than the other. Long ago, martial arts experts understood that to preserve a strong balance, they must have their legs spread and never on the same line.

The length of the stirrup leather can vary in accordance with the horse's conformation and the rider's size. But when learning to jump, it is always best to shorten it in such a way that the stirrup base is level with the ankle joint when the rider's legs are hanging. (See Fig. 28.) Furthermore, when the stirrups are shorter, the rider has more strength and better fixity with the legs. If a rider has one leg that is weaker than the other, it is wise to shorten the stirrup leather one or two holes on the side of the weak leg to strengthen it.

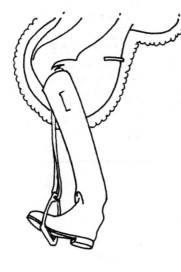 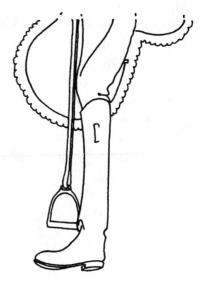

FIG. 28

Each stirrup iron should be almost perpendicular to the horse's body, with the outside branch pointing slightly forward. In the case of an increase of weight in your heels, your toes will turn inward. In the reverse situation, they would turn outward and weaken the leg action. Also, inside your boots, you should curl your toes just as if they were directly in contact with the stirrup irons, trying to hold the bases.

Clothing . . . there is so much to say on this subject. Why, in practicing the most noble sport, are people so negligent about the way they dress? I think that I found a satisfactory answer to this question. One day I heard a line that I have slightly modified. "If a rider is poorly dressed, he/she will be noticed by his/her neglectful appearance. But if a rider is properly dressed, he/she will be noticed for his/her ability to ride." The choice is now yours, but please, let people know that they should dress in accordance with the sport.

Insofar as the shoes are concerned, it is a matter of safety. *Do not* ride a horse with flat soles, such as sneakers or tennis shoes. Paddock boots and riding boots are so much more comfortable to ride with and safe as can be because they have heels and no loose parts that can catch on the stirrup irons.

To develop and improve fixity, suppleness, and balance in the jumping position, stretch the muscles of both your lower body and upper body using the exercises listed below. They should be done with shorter

EXERCISES for the RIDER

stirrups, first at the halt and then at the walk, trot, and canter.

The Forward Position

You can educate your body to move properly and to maintain the correct forward position over fences with the following exercises. In this simple progression, each phase should be repeated several times before moving on to the next.

A. Keeping your upper body straight and erect, increase the weight in your heels. Allow your legs to move forward and *push* your heels down until your seat SLIDES backward toward the cantle of the saddle while allowing your legs to move forward. (See Fig. 29A, next page.)

B. In the same manner, slide your seat back, but this time, as you proceed, increase the pressure of your calves against the horse's barrel so that you do not allow your legs to move forward. (See Fig. 29B.)

C. Slide your seat backward, now letting your upper body lower forward above the horse's neck as naturally as possible. (See Fig. 29C.)

D. Slide into the forward position without leaning on the horse's neck with your hands, but keeping them slightly above his neck, making believe that you are holding the reins. (See Fig. 29D.)

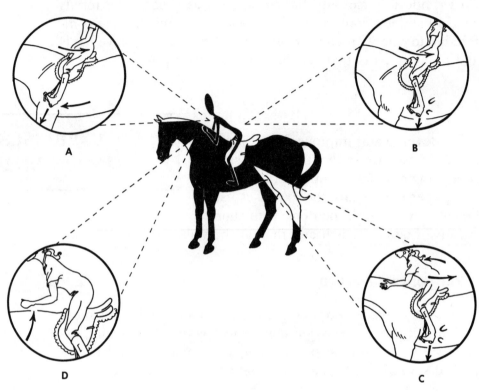

FIG. 29

The HANDBOOK of JUMPING ESSENTIALS

Lower Body Exercises

1. Standing straight, sink all your weight into your heels. At first hold onto the horse's mane or a neck strap and then, progressively, balance on your own. (See Fig. 30.)

2. Stand straight on your toes with your heels as high as possible, holding onto the mane at first to help you, and then, progressively, balance on your own. (See Fig. 31.)

Every time you practice these exercises, remain in this position as long as you are able and try to beat your own record every time. These two exercises should be alternated and also done with your arms crossed behind your back.

FIG. 30

FIG. 31

Upper Body Exercises

While practicing these exercises, your legs must be tight and remain at the girth without sliding forward or backward. The following exercises should be done equally with the right and then the left hand, the reins remaining in the resting hand.

1. Assume the forward position and touch your right toe with your right hand. To lower your upper body, first tighten your calves and then slide your seat backward. (See Fig. 32.)

FIG. 32

FIG. 33

FIG. 34

2. In the forward position, touch your left toe with your right hand passing under your left arm. Increase the pressure of your lower legs to make certain they remain in place. (See Fig. 33.)

3. Sitting down, with your right hand passing in front of your abdomen and under your left arm, rotate your upper body to reach and grab the cantle of the saddle. (See Fig. 34.)

4. Sitting down, with your right hand passing behind your back, twist your upper body to touch the pommel of the saddle (or as close to it as you can reach). Make certain that your lower legs stay in place. (See Fig. 35.)

5. Standing slightly, passing your right hand between your upper legs, grab the cantle of the saddle and hold for a moment. Avoid leaning on the horse's back with your left hand. (See Fig. 36.)

For best results, all the exercises of the lower and upper body should be combined and executed with progressively faster cadence. For example, quickly switch from

FIG. 35

FIG. 36

The HANDBOOK of JUMPING ESSENTIALS

sitting to standing on your heels, to the forward position, to standing on your toes, and back to the sitting position. When these exercises become easy at a standstill, they should be practiced at the walk, trot, and at the canter.

Part 1: Learning to Maintain the Forward Position

To easily learn or follow this simple step-by-step progression, you should have at your disposal what people call "a made horse" or a good school horse that will execute the work without any hesitation. Remember this old adage:

"To young riders, old horses, to old riders, young horses."

With your Gentil Helper, set up a line of obstacles on the track of the ring. To do this, you must first lay across the track a single rail on the ground at the beginning of the long side. Pace 9 feet (three steps) and then lay three rails together with one standard on either side. Then pace another 18 feet (six steps) and do the same. Pace another 21 feet (seven steps) and place one more set of rails and standards. Finally, pace 24 feet (eight steps) and set up your last obstacle. (See Fig. 37.)

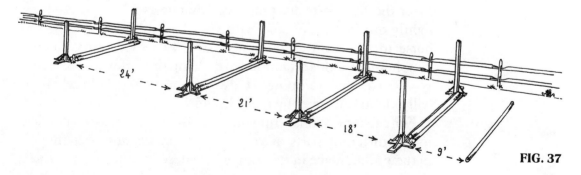

FIG. 37

On your horse, walk a few times through the line, and when he is absolutely relaxed, trot back and forth over it. It is recommended to practice the exercises of the lower and upper body while you are walking and trotting over the line. Then, starting with the last set of rails and standards, successively build the crossrails (18 inches high) after each couple of passages. (See Fig. 38.)

To accomplish this type of schooling and be successful, you must ride your approach at the posting trot. At 5 to 6 feet before the rail on the ground (it would be a good idea to put two markers at this point), sit to the trot and immediately shift your weight to your heels. Near the same rail, smoothly switch to the forward position and maintain it.

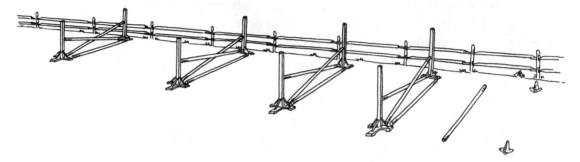

FIG. 38

At the trot, jump over the first crossrail and allow your horse to canter the following three fences by himself. The premeasured distances between the crossrails will assure a comfortable takeoff spot for the horse. In between the jumps, also maintain the forward position without bringing your upper body back up. After the last obstacle, progressively raise your upper body, sit lightly on the saddle, and with your legs in contact, bring your horse to a halt for a moment or two. For a long time to come you should use this technique to develop the reflex of rebalancing your horse after jumping. It also will be a great help when you will ride an entire course of obstacles.

For each individual trip you jump over the line, BE ATTENTIVE to the different parts of your body to make sure that they are in the proper place in function of the described forward position. With repetition, it will soon become a habit, and you will not have to think about it any more.

To do so, ride as follows (see Fig. 39):

SEAT: slightly out of the saddle, directly above your feet. Your upper body is almost parallel to the horse's neck.

The HANDBOOK of JUMPING ESSENTIALS

LEGS: at the girth, in tight contact with the horse's barrel.

HANDS: relaxed and in soft contact with the horse's neck.

FIG. 39

THESE EXERCISES WILL DEVELOP YOUR

- Proper balance.
- Fixity of the legs.
- Self-confidence.
- Relaxation of the mind and body.

HELPFUL SUGGESTIONS

While you are going over the line, concentrate on your feet to make sure that your heels are down and your toes are up. Nevertheless, do not break your ankles with excess flexion, or you will lose the benefit of these shock absorbers by locking the joints. Concentrating on raising your toes will be sufficient to preserve the proper foot position.

To avoid surprising the horse by a sudden leg action, always maintain a steady contact with your calves.

First, jump the line holding onto the mane or a neck strap. Second, learn to softly hold the reins with your two hands, and then with only one. Finally, jump the line without holding onto the reins at all.

Practice, also, to move your hands forward over each jump, to release the contact with the horse's mouth and to allow him to jump freely.

When you are jumping the line, pick a focal point far away in front of you and look at it, focusing between the horse's ears.

For best results, to progress rapidly and to learn to sustain the forward position, you must frequently practice all the exercises of the lower and upper body mentioned above *while jumping* low fences.

Part 2: Learning to Develop Strength and Good Timing in Your Lower Legs

In my opinion, one of the fastest, the safest, and the most interesting ways to strengthen and develop good timing in your lower legs is to jump WITHOUT STIRRUP IRONS, SITTING DOWN in the saddle.

With your Gentil Helper, across the track set four rails together on the ground with one standard on either side.

At a distance from the rails, pick up the sitting trot and proceed as follows (see Fig. 40):

A. Several times trot back and forth over the rails on the ground, MAINTAINING YOUR SITTING POSITION. Practice to tighten your lower legs as you go over the rails, i.e., from the takeoff to the landing phase.

B. Set up an 18-inch crossrail and proceed in the same manner: Do not lean forward, but maintain your upper body constantly erect.

SEAT: in contact with the saddle *at all times*.

LEGS: tight at the girth when the horse approaches, jumps, and lands after the obstacle.

HANDS: one hand holding onto the pommel to secure your balance and to "glue" your seat to the saddle; the other hand relaxed, holding long reins.

FIG. 40

With practice, as your lower legs become stronger and tighter, you will hold onto the pommel less and less until you will not need it any more and are even able to jump with your arms crossed behind your back. Soon you will realize that you are capable of jumping any size fence, combinations, and even courses.

THIS EXERCISE WILL

• Definitely develop the reflex to tighten your lower legs as the horse takes off until after the landing.

• Teach you to relax your upper body and soften your hands.

• Teach you to look straight ahead.

• Build the greatest self-confidence in your abilities to ride as well as help you to control your balance in case of a surprising buck from the horse.

When you are comfortable jumping without stirrup irons sitting down, it will become very easy to learn to jump leaning forward without stirrup irons. To do so, at a distance, pick up the trot and direct your horse toward the obstacle. As you approach, slightly raise your lower legs, making believe that you actually still have your stirrup irons.

SEAT: slightly out of the saddle, directly above your feet.

LEGS: tight at the girth, with your knees and your toes raised.

HANDS: relaxed, in soft contact with the horse's mouth.

HELPFUL SUGGESTION

To feel very comfortable jumping without stirrup irons while sitting or leaning forward, you need to jump many obstacles, beginning with low ones and gradually, as you feel more confident, increasing the height and width.

This work should also be done at a steady canter.

Part 3: Learning to Develop the Timing of Your Upper Body

One of the fastest ways to perfect the timing of your upper body is to jump low fences following the pattern of a circle.

With your Gentil Helper, set up a crossrail or a low vertical about 2 feet in height in the middle of the ring (see Fig. 41):

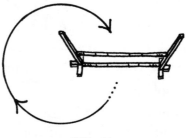

FIG. 41

Pick up the trot and maintain this gait on a circle with a radius of about 20 feet. Every revolution, jump the obstacle as follows (see Fig. 42):

A. Before the jump:

SEAT: light in the saddle, your upper body leaning slightly forward.

LEGS: acting together at the girth to maintain the impulsion.

HANDS: in soft contact with the horse's mouth, preserving good balance.

B. Over the jump: hold the forward position.

C. After the jump:

SEAT: light in the saddle, with your upper body coming back up promptly, but smoothly.

LEGS: acting stronger at the girth to re-engage the horse's hind legs.

HANDS: resisting together to rebalance the horse.

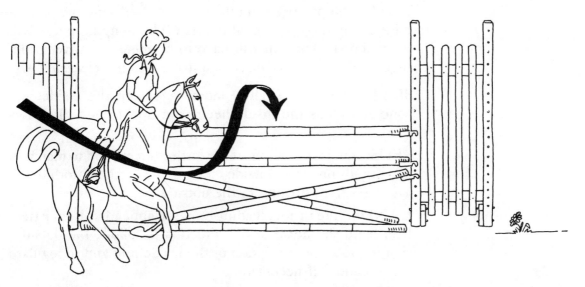

FIG. 42

While practicing this exercise, always preserve the gait and the same size circle. At the beginning, the horse may give you awkward jumps, but no matter how disunited he may be approaching the obstacle, let him jump over it. With time, he will learn to set himself for the best spot and also always land on the proper lead. It is understood that this gymnastic should be practiced tracking to the right as well as tracking to the left.

THIS EXERCISE WILL TEACH YOU

- To always be alert and attentive.
- To look where you are going.
- To follow a pattern.
- To maintain the horse's balance.
- To create and to sustain the impulsion.
- To keep your upper body *relaxed* and *ready* to follow the motion without preceding it.
- To develop your reflexes and to perfect the timing of your legs.

You also will practice a similar exercise, following the pattern of a figure eight (two tangent circles). The jumping phase will be very similar, but you will have to be more attentive to the changes of direction. To do so, approach the obstacle as follows:

SEAT: light with slightly more weight on the inside seat bone as well as the inside heel; your upper body tilted forward.

LEGS: the inside acting at the girth to create and to maintain the impulsion; the outside behind the girth to forbid the haunches from drifting to the outside.

HANDS: the inside, leading rein (see appendix, Rein Effect I) to bend the horse in the direction to follow; the outside, yielding to allow the action of the inside rein and to regulate the direction, if necessary.

THIS EXERCISE WILL TEACH YOU

- To turn and to maintain the haunches toward the inside of the circle.
- To sustain the forward motion and the impulsion.

- To keep the same radius and to follow a pattern.
- To bend the horse in the direction to follow.

HELPFUL SUGGESTIONS

At the takeoff phase, you may apply the aids for the canter departure to obtain the opposite lead, but this procedure is not foolproof.

If your horse has the tendency to fall into the turns, equalize your weight directly above the saddle, keep the same pressure on each stirrup iron, and be ready to support him with an appropriate inside indirect rein (see appendix, Rein Effect III), reinforced by stronger legs.

After you have become familiar with this type of work, it would be wise to often vary the diameter of the circles to bigger, smaller, and to an oval shape. (See Fig. 43.)

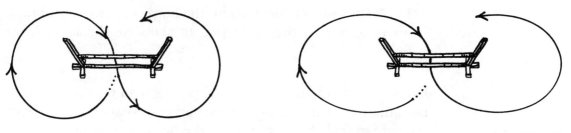

FIG. 43

Good turns are fundamental and even crucial to follow the pattern of a jumping course, to approach an obstacle properly from the correct angle, and to maintain the horse's engagement for balance.

Part 4: Learning to Hold the Forward Position between Two Obstacles

With your Gentil Helper, you will construct a low crossrail obstacle about 2 feet in height on the track. Then pace 18 to 21 feet (six to seven paces) and build a low vertical 2 feet high.

Away from the combination, pick up the posting trot. After

you have established balance, rhythm, and impulsion, approach the two obstacles. At about 30 feet before the crossrail, sit to the trot, shift your weight down to your heels, and adopt the forward position. Then trot over the first element and allow your horse to jump the second obstacle by himself. The purpose of the crossrail is to incite your horse to pick up the canter. The predetermined distance will impel him to jump the vertical fence from a comfortable takeoff spot.

In between the obstacles, hold the forward position and focus on the middle of the top rail.

SEAT: out of the saddle, directly above your feet. The upper body is slightly tilted forward in a *passive* attitude.

LEGS: acting together at the girth to maintain the impulsion, and then tight against the horse's sides from the takeoff phase until the landing.

HANDS: in soft contact with the horse's mouth to maintain his balance and then releasing to allow the horse to jump freely.

Do not try to influence what is happening with your upper body but rather go with the motion, adopting a passive position and learning to feel the inertia when the horse is jumping.

After several trials, progressively raise the vertical 3 inches by 3 inches until it reaches about 3 feet 6 inches in height. When the horse lands, allow him to canter three to four strides on a straight line before you bring him to a halt (using only your natural aids). On this subject—avoid using the ring fencing for stopping the horse. It is only an instructor's easy method to get the job done, and it does not teach you anything. Besides, one day, on the spur of a funny mood, your horse may very well jump this fencing too . . . .

When you feel at ease jumping the vertical, it will be time to transform it to a low oxer type of fence about 2 feet square. To keep a similar feeling when you jump this new obstacle, make sure that when you build it, the exact placement of the vertical corresponds with the center of the oxer. (See Fig. 20, page 21.)

After a few trips, widen the oxer to 3 feet and raise the back rail to 2 feet 3 inches. Then, as you practice, continue raising the two rails until the back one reaches 3 feet 6 inches and the front 3 feet 3 inches.

When you are absolutely comfortable in this gymnastic, square the oxer to 3 feet 6 inches in height and 3 feet 6 inches in width.

With practice and time, you should be able to jump this trotting combination in the forward position without holding the reins (see Fig. 44) and, furthermore, without your stirrup irons.

FIG. 44

THIS EXERCISE WILL

• Familiarize you with the takeoff spot without being concerned about adjusting the stride.

• Help you to realize what a comfortable distance feels like.

- Help you see the difference in the approach between a vertical and an oxer type of obstacle.
- Teach you to coordinate your natural aids.
- Improve your balance.
- Build your self-confidence.

HELPFUL SUGGESTIONS

If you feel tension, to help you to relax, breathe SLOWLY and DEEPLY several times; inhale through the nose and exhale through the mouth. Your being at ease is very important because this feeling will be transmitted to your horse.

If you get left behind the motion, instead of pulling on the horse's mouth, develop the reflex to tighten your legs, soften your hands, and lower your seat closer to the saddle to regain your balance.

Part 5: Learning to Switch from a Forward Position to a Half Seat

Add a third element to the in-and-out combination. To do so, pace five strides (about 72 feet) and build a vertical about 3 feet high.

Away from the combination, pick up the posting trot. After you have established balance, rhythm, and impulsion, aim your horse toward the three obstacles. About 25 feet before the cross-rail, sit to the trot, shift your weight down to your heels, and adopt the forward position. Then trot over the first element and allow the horse to freely jump the second. Afterward, support him with your legs and hands to approach and clear the new vertical element. After the third jump, let your horse canter three to four strides before bringing him to a halt.

In between the second and the third obstacle, your natural aids are:

SEAT: closer to the saddle, the upper body slightly coming back up, but ready to go forward again to meet the third fence.

LEGS: acting together at the girth to preserve the impulsion.

HANDS: taking a soft contact with the horse's mouth to maintain his balance.

If you feel lost or like a blind person and do not see the spot for the third obstacle, do not be concerned. The distance between the fences is predetermined, and if you sustain the pace, your horse will meet a comfortable takeoff spot. Time and practice will develop your sense of feel and your aptitude to see the distance.

As soon as you are comfortable with this distance, you will be able to change it and begin to be more active in your riding.

Progressively, open the distance a few inches to about 3 feet (75 feet total) to learn to lengthen the horse's stride to meet the distant spot:

FIG. 45

SEAT: light, but close to the saddle.

LEGS: acting together at the girth, *stronger, but not faster*, to lengthen the strides and not rush him.

HANDS: slightly releasing together to allow freedom of the motion.

Progressively, reduce the distance from about 3 feet (69 feet total) to a few inches to learn to shorten the horse's stride to meet a closer spot:

SEAT: light, in contact with the saddle.

LEGS: acting and releasing together at the girth to maintain the engagement.

HANDS: resisting together to shorten the strides. A discreet half-halt may be necessary (see Chapter Three, page 115).

As you please, you may also change the last obstacle to a low oxer and gradually increase its width and height.

THIS LINE OF THREE OBSTACLES WILL TEACH YOU

- To easily switch from the forward position to the half seat.
- To educate your sense of feel about striding and the pace.
- To be active with your legs to lengthen the strides.
- To resist with your hands to shorten the strides.
- To improve your balance and develop your self-confidence.

HELPFUL SUGGESTIONS

If, during the approach, you change your body position too suddenly, you will disturb the horse's balance. When you have the opportunity, step on a scale and check your weight. . . . From a standing position, quickly drop to sit on your heels: observe that when you are going down, your weight will lessen about 10 to 20 pounds. From this sitting position, do the opposite and quickly rise to stand again: also, notice that when you are going up, your weight will increase about 10 to 30 pounds. You may easily conclude that while moving fast, down or up, your weight decreases or increases. Imagine now, for an instant, if you were to suddenly change position, how your horse would feel when he is properly balanced and ready to go over a jump.

While jumping an obstacle, if your horse touches the rail with his forelegs, the cause is very often from your hands leaning too much on his neck. If your horse touches the rails with his hind legs, the cause is very often from your seat being behind the motion.

Part 6: Learning to Switch from a Forward to a Sitting Position

Now you will move the third obstacle and place it on the centerline parallel to the fencing of the ring. The pacing between the second and the third obstacle will follow the pattern of a smooth curved line and be about 84 feet in length (seven strides at a 90-degree angle). (See Fig. 46.)

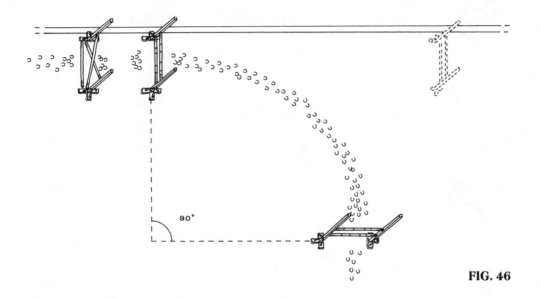

FIG. 46

Away from the combination, pick up the posting trot. After you have established balance, rhythm, and impulsion, lead the horse toward the crossrail. At about 20 feet before the takeoff, sit to the trot, shift your weight down to your heels, and adopt the forward position. Then trot over the first element and allow the horse to freely jump the next.

As you take off to jump the second fence, turn your head and focus on the third obstacle and seek a comfortable takeoff spot. When you land, smoothly and promptly bring your upper body to an upright position just as if you were riding on the flat, and simultaneously negotiate your turn toward the third obstacle as follows (see Fig. 47) (this turn will be to the right, but it would be the opposite if it were to the left):

FIG. 47

SEAT: upper body erect, but *light* in the saddle to help the horse to rebalance himself.

LEGS: the right is active at the girth to maintain the forward motion; the left resists behind the girth to forbid the haunches from drifting to the left.

HANDS: first resist together, and then the right leading rein (see appendix, Rein Effect I) and the left yielding to allow and then regulate the action of the right rein.

As soon as you have completed the turn, prepare your forward position to meet the third obstacle. After this last jump, do not forget to always bring your horse to a halt.

THE EXERCISE WITH A CURVED LINE WILL TEACH YOU

• To shift your weight smoothly and promptly from the forward to the sitting position and back to the forward position.

• To look very attentively and follow a pattern.

• To make a quick decision when you see a spot.

• To coordinate your legs and hands to rebalance the horse and to negotiate a turn.

• To develop your self-confidence.

HELPFUL SUGGESTIONS

While you are turning to meet the next obstacle, if you see a long spot, do not run for it, but instead wait one more stride for a quieter distance.

If you think that your spot is a little too long, you may close the turn and find a better takeoff spot, or if you think that your spot is much too long, you may widen your turn and add another stride. (See Fig. 48A.)

If you think that your spot is a little too short, you may widen the turn and find a better takeoff spot, or if you think that your spot is much too short, you may close your turn and leave one stride out. (See Fig. 48B.)

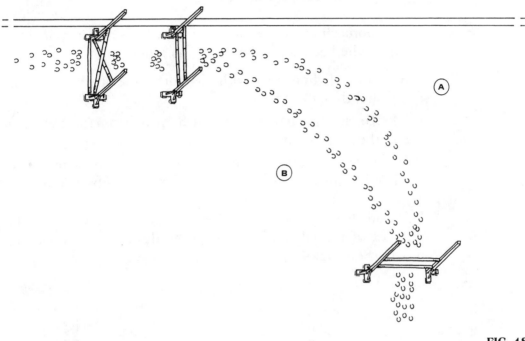

FIG. 48

Part 7: Learning to Approach a Single Obstacle at the Canter

It is time now to remove the crossrail from the combination, to let the upright obstacle stand by itself on the track.

Away from the obstacle, pick up the canter on a circle and

immediately establish balance, rhythm, and impulsion. Then leave the circle and ride toward the fence.

To approach a vertical, you must look for an average spot; then focus on the top rail and ride as follows:

SEAT: in light contact with the saddle, upper body leaning slightly forward.

LEGS: active at the girth to maintain the impulsion and the engagement.

HANDS: in soft contact with the horse's mouth, ready to act if the horse's balance changes.

To approach an oxer, you must look for a closer spot; then focus on the back top rail and ride as follows:

SEAT: in light contact with the saddle, the upper body leaning slightly more forward.

LEGS: acting together at the girth, to maintain the impulsion and the engagement.

HANDS: in very light contact with the horse's mouth to allow him to extend and come closer to the obstacle base.

It is said that an obstacle has been properly jumped when the distance of the takeoff is equal to the distance of the landing phase. (See Fig. 49.)

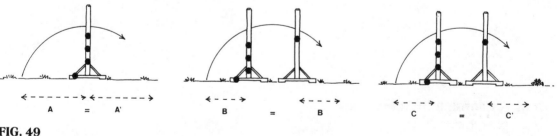

FIG. 49

Most jumping problems come either from the rider's or the horse's balance. If you have a mediocre approach, interrupt your action and ride another circle, making sure that your own balance is correct, and then send the horse "in front of your legs" (obediently) to re-establish the pace and the balance ("behind your legs" means the horse is reluctant to respond to the actions of your legs).

As you approach an obstacle, after finding your spot, always aim for the center and focus on the top rail (it will be the back one for an oxer). If you focus at the base, it may incite the horse to come too close to the obstacle and make him take off from too tight a spot.

To approach, jump, and turn after an obstacle, follow the same technique as the one described in Part 6, above.

In any case, after a jump, always remember to rebalance your horse.

THIS EXERCISE WITH A SINGLE FENCE WILL

- Teach you to concentrate on the balance, the rhythm, and the impulsion.
- Perfect your own balance and your position.
- Teach you to wait and seek a spot.
- Prepare you to jump a course of obstacles.

HELPFUL SUGGESTIONS

You have to see how far away you are from the takeoff spot in order to make a correction to the stride. Do not be concerned if you cannot see the distance. Time and practice will develop your aptitude to better observe. In the meantime, concentrate on your position, the horse's balance, the rhythm, and the impulsion.

When you see a distance, wait one more stride and confirm what you saw before making an adjustment.

When you see a long spot, avoid running for it but discipline yourself to wait for a quieter distance.

If you see a distance, but are not sure whether to lengthen or shorten the strides, *do neither*, but maintain balance, rhythm, and impulsion.

Part 8: Learning to Approach
an In-and-Out Combination

With your Gentil Helper, build two simple vertical obstacles about 3 feet high on the track and measure 22 to 24 feet (seven to eight paces) in between.

At a distance from the combination, pick up the canter and, just as you did before, establish the balance, the rhythm, and the impulsion. Then leave the circle and ride toward the in-and-out.

To approach the first element, look for a normal takeoff spot; then focus on the top of the second obstacle and ride as follows:

SEAT: in light contact with the saddle, the upper body leaning slightly forward.

LEGS: active at the girth to maintain the impulsion and the engagement.

HANDS: in soft contact with the horse's mouth and ready to resist if the horse leans on the bit too much.

To jump an in-and-out combination does not present any special complications. The only difficulty consists of finding the proper takeoff spot for the first element. If you do, you will have a very smooth ride. But if you err, you will have either a too long or too short takeoff spot and will have to adjust.

If you are too long: as you jump the first element, establish a contact with the horse's mouth and, as soon as you have landed, ride STRONGER, but not FASTER, with your legs to also jump the second obstacle from a long spot.

If you are too short: as you have landed after the first element, you will have to resist with your hands to forbid the horse to lengthen the stride and then loosen the reins so that you will be able to jump the second obstacle from a short spot also.

To jump an in-and-out combination of a vertical to an oxer, you should look for a long spot as you approach the first element and ride forward all the way through. To jump an in-and-out combination of an oxer to a vertical, you should look for a closer spot and steady the pace in between.(See Fig. 50.)

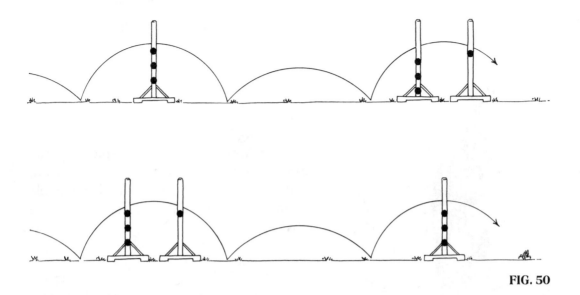

FIG. 50

THIS EXERCISE WILL

- Develop your eyes to see the spots.
- Help you to ride according to what you see.
- Enable you to act effectively with your legs and hands.
- Perfect your balance.

HELPFUL SUGGESTIONS

When you ride a course, if you know that the distance in between the two obstacles is long, you will have to smoothly approach the first element with a long stride and lengthen as you land. If you know that the distance is short, you will have to approach the first element with a short stride and shorten in between.

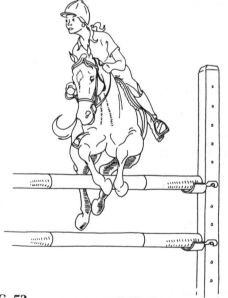

FIG. 51

Part 9: Learning to Turn before, on Top of, and after the Obstacle

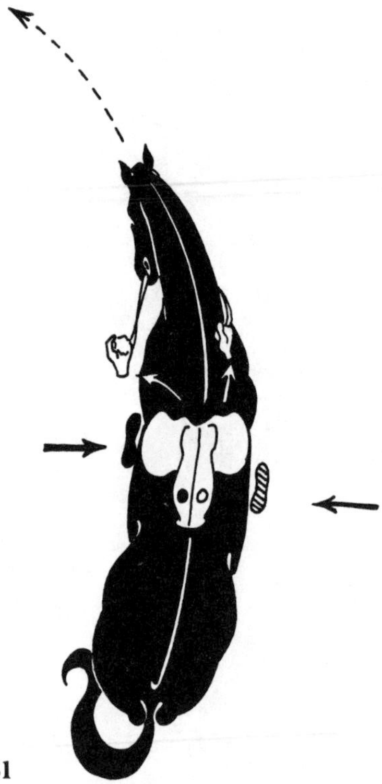

You will now need an obstacle about 3 feet to 3 feet 6 inches high in the middle of the ring.

Away from this obstacle, pick up the canter, establish the balance, the rhythm, and the impulsion. Then widen the circle to meet the curved path leading to the obstacle.

During the approach, look for your spot and ride as follows (see Fig. 51):

SEAT: in light contact with the saddle with more weight on the inside seat bone.

LEGS: the inside leg acts at the girth to create and to maintain the impulsion; the outside leg acts behind the girth to prevent and forbid the haunches from drifting toward the outside of the circle.

HANDS: the inside hand acts with a leading rein (see appendix, Rein Effect I); the outside hand yields to allow the action of the inside rein but is ready to act, either to push the horse's shoulders with a neck rein (see appendix, Rein Effect III) or to regulate the balance by resisting.

At all times, make sure that your horse remains "straight" (the two lateral bipeds are parallel), engaged, and balanced.

On top of the obstacle, keep looking where you are going and ride as follows (see Fig. 52):

SEAT: out of the saddle, directly above

FIG. 52

your feet, with more weight on your inside stirrup iron.

LEGS: the inside leg is active and very slightly behind the girth to push the haunches toward the outside; the outside leg is passive to allow the action of the inside (these special leg actions are executed to facilitate the turn).

HANDS: the inside hand is active using a leading rein (see appendix, Rein Effect I); the outside hand is passive to allow the action of the inside rein.

As you land, smoothly and promptly raise your upper body and bring your seat closer to the saddle. As you re-establish the horse's balance, still look where you are going and continue using the same aids to complete the turn.

THIS EXERCISE WILL TEACH YOU

- To approach the obstacle to meet a longer or closer spot.
- To maintain your horse's balance and straightness.
- To look where you are going and follow a pattern.
- To better coordinate your aids.
- To save time while you are riding a course.

HELPFUL SUGGESTIONS

As you practice the turns, you should vary the radius of the circle to create a different sort of challenge each time. It also will be wise to use the same technique to practice the turns while jumping oxers and a combination of two obstacles.

If your horse has a tendency to cut the turns short, you should forbid him with a stronger leg action and a firm inside indirect rein (see appendix, Rein Effect III). To prevent this so common fault, you should practice widening and narrowing circles on the flat, using your inside or outside lateral aids. First at the walk and then at the trot and canter, establish a circle with about a 15-foot radius. To widen the circle, always maintaining the horse's spinal column PARALLEL to the original circle pattern, you will ride as follows:

SEAT: more weight on your outside seat bone.

LEGS: the inside leg acts behind the girth to displace the haunches toward the outside; the outside leg acts at the girth to create and to maintain the impulsion and the engagement.

HANDS: the inside hand acts with an indirect rein (see appendix, Rein Effect III), to push the forehand to the outside; the outside hand yields and then regulates the action of the inside rein. (See Fig. 53A.)

To narrow the circle, reverse your aids, i.e., more weight on the inside seat bone, outside leg behind the girth, outside indirect rein (see appendix, Rein Effect III). (See Fig. 53B.) At first you will realize that it is much easier to widen than to narrow the circles. Knowing this, concentrate at the beginning to widen in both directions, to the left and the right. After practicing for two or three days, reverse the process and notice that it is now easier to reduce the size of the circle. Alternating promptly from a wide circle to a narrow one and vice versa, will develop good balance and a keener response from your horse.(See Fig. 53.)

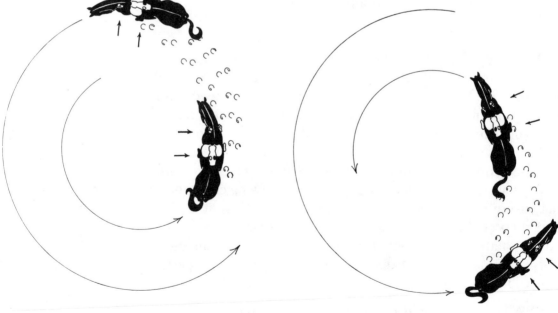

FIG. 53   A   B

The HANDBOOK of JUMPING ESSENTIALS

Part 10: Learning to Jump a Course

A course is simply the succession of obstacles one after another that is displayed on a pattern made of straight lines and curves.

Whether you intend to ride in *hunter*, *equitation*, or *jumper* classes, the fundamental rules remain very similar. The difference is a matter of pace, patterns, tightness in the turns, and the height of the obstacles.

At this point in your progression, you already have rehearsed segments of typical courses and have learned most of the basics to successfully ride in the style you may have chosen.

When you are about to jump a course, you will have to concentrate on two important points: to learn and memorize the course and the warm-up phase.

LEARNING THE COURSE

At a horse show, before mounting your horse, your first task as a rider is to concentrate on the posted chart where the course is drawn and to memorize the order of the various obstacles. Whether or not you are authorized to walk the actual course, you have to take a good look at the obstacles to jump. You should observe them from all the possible angles along the rail (see Fig. 54A), and from the top of the grandstand, if there is

A   B   **FIG. 54**

one, (see Fig. 54B); a line or a turn may not appear as equal from one side to another, and you must be aware of this fact *before* entering the ring.

As you observe the "route" to follow, you will plan and repeat in your mind the successive decisions you will have to make to negotiate a good course.

To help you to memorize the layout and your strategy, it will be a good idea to find a nearby flat area. Imagine that your course is set on it and at the trot ride the pattern you will have to follow. As you do so, think about each particular obstacle, each line, each turn, and every decision as if you actually were cantering the real course.

THE WARM-UP

If you are an "educated rider" or on the way to becoming one, you must realize that before mounting your horse, it is always wise to stretch your limbs and to bend your joints to eliminate your physical stiffness. Take a few minutes and, in a corner, do exercises, such as touching your toes without bending your knees, one after the other, lifting your knees up to your chest, sitting on your heels, etc. These exercises, I call . . . *light* Aerobic. (See Fig. 55.)

FIG. 55

When your muscles are loose and limbered, it will be time to mount your horse and think about his body.

For a few minutes, walk him around and observe his mood. This will tell you how to begin, but in general, you will trot 5 to 10 minutes—and do not forget to canter on one lead and then the other. If your horse has some knowledge of lateral work, most often called dressage, incorporate it in the warm up. Do not hesitate to go through what he needs to loosen up, especially concentrating on his stiff side. Do not forget the transitions, the halts, the rein back, and the lengthening and shortening of the strides. These exercises, I now call—Equi-robic. (See Fig. 56.)

FIG. 56

Then leg him up over a few crossrails before jumping verticals and oxers. Always begin jumping from a trot to preserve the leg tendons. Avoid jumping too much so that you will save his energy. Nevertheless, you should manage to go over five to ten obstacles as well as one or two combinations or lines.

Before you are about to enter the ring, stand near the entrance gate, observe several riders going around the course, and one more time recite your plan in your mind.

Enter the ring with a *positive* attitude and, with an energetic trot, quickly reach your starting circle. Bring your horse to a slower trot or even to a walk and immediately pick up the canter: the promptness of his response will indicate whether or not his attention is yours. Then establish the pace, the impulsion, and the balance. As you leave the circle, look for your first takeoff spot and then focus on the center of the top rail.

Ride your entire course *breathing with calmness* and execute your strategy, step-by-step, according to your plan and your knowledge. Remember that it is most important to maintain both your own and your horse's balance. To do so, ride as follows:

ON THE FLAT, BETWEEN THE OBSTACLES

SEAT: in light contact with the saddle, directly above your feet; but, remember, leaning your upper body forward or backward will increase or decrease, respectively, the horse's speed.

LEGS: at the girth act, resist, or yield to produce and to maintain the horse's forward motion, increase the speed, engage the hindquarters, as well as create and sustain the impulsion; behind the girth action of one leg will displace or forbid the haunches from drifting.

HANDS: act, resist, or yield through the reins to regulate the forward motion, to maintain the balance, and to turn.

BEFORE THE OBSTACLE

SEAT: in light contact with the saddle, in balance above your feet.

LEGS: acting together to engage the hindquarters.

HANDS: in soft contact with the horse's mouth to sustain his balance.

OVER THE OBSTACLE

SEAT: out of the saddle, directly above your feet.

LEGS: tight to maintain stability and impulsion.

HANDS: yield to allow the horse to stretch his top line.

LANDING AFTER THE OBSTACLE

SEAT: comes closer to the saddle and the upper body rises slightly.

LEGS: acting together to re-engage the hindquarters.

HANDS: yield first and then act to re-establish the horse's balance.

IN THE TURNS

SEAT: more weight on the inside stirrup iron.

LEGS: inside leg at the girth to maintain the impulsion; outside leg behind the girth to forbid the haunches from drifting.

HANDS: inside hand leading to indicate the direction to follow; outside hand yielding to allow the action of the inside rein and then to regulate.

Also, make sure that the horse follows the pattern of the course. If he drifts, make a discreet correction with your indirect rein (see appendix, Rein Effect III) and the corresponding leg, i.e., if he drifts to the left, use your left leg and hand action, vice versa for the right.

JUMPING A COURSE WILL

• Test your riding skills, abilities to think, and your knowledge.

• Develop your "dynamic spirit" (desire to accomplish).

• Develop your self-confidence.

• Familiarize you with horse shows' expectations.

• Bring you many satisfactions.

HELPFUL SUGGESTIONS

If, at some point, you lose control of the pace, immediately think, "This is simply flat work," and resolve the situation calmly as you would if you were not riding a jumping course.

Ride all your fences, including the *very last one*, which is too often neglected. Your course, in fact, begins and ends when you enter and leave the ring.

Use all your turns to perfect the balance and the control of your horse.

For the turns on the flat, it is best to ride them holding the inside canter lead, but if you or your horse are not knowledge-able enough to obtain flying changes of lead when required, concentrate on maintaining a smooth counter-canter with your inside leg acting behind the girth. If your horse cross-canters (i.e., left lead with the forelegs and right lead for the hind legs or vice versa), simply send him forward with a stronger leg action and apply the aids for the correct canter lead.

If you encounter a problem, think that it is already behind you and concentrate on what is in FRONT OF YOU to prevent new mistakes.

If you feel tense or maybe nervous, take several deep breaths. Just like anyone, you may have some mental fears. Time will eliminate them, but you must control the physical ones. Your personal relaxation is most important because it will directly affect the horse's state of mind and his attitude.

To learn to steady the pace and to control your ability to breathe in cadence while you are jumping a course, it will be a good idea when you are at home to jump many courses and, as you go around, *count out loud* all the horse's strides during the entire progression.

Avoid riding with your fingers tight on the reins, or you will unconsciously shorten the strides and, as a result, see only short spots. Instead, try to constantly release the contact when your horse is balanced.

To develop your attention span and keen reflexes, it is a good gymnastic to jump a course, asking your Gentil Helper to guide you by calling out loud which obstacles to jump next by surprise!

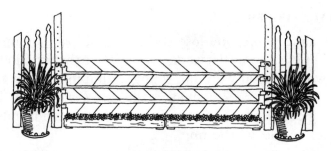

FIG. 57 Vertical obstacle with planks

The HANDBOOK of JUMPING ESSENTIALS

Three

The EDUCATION of the HORSE

Before introducing the schooling over fences, it would be to your best advantage to first inculcate the basic flat work movements to your horse.

HOW MUCH SHOULD YOUR HORSE KNOW?

Many good opinions have been uttered on this topic, but provided that your horse is over three years of age and your progression plan is gradual, you may begin the study over fences.

Nevertheless, my advice is: to avoid long-term tribulations, your horse should have enough training on the flat to respond to your leg and hand actions, beyond any doubts. It will be better and so much safer if he were very obedient at the walk, trot, canter and able to easily switch from one gait to another while retaining adequate balance, rhythm, and a sufficient impulsion.

The rest will improve or be instilled in time, considering that, to avoid fatigue and also boredom, you will seldom jump every day. There will be plenty of time to pursue and to perfect the schooling on the flat.

To reach your goals, in these simple progressions, the different lessons should be repeated until the horse has no more apprehension and always works with a calm attitude and a good balance.

LEARNING to START a HORSE over FENCES

Jumping is very natural for the horse. But to perform to the best of his abilities, freedom of his head and neck is a must. To give a horse the perfect opportunity to begin learning properly, one of the most successful methods will be to use the longe line to allow him to jump at semiliberty.

Once the horse has understood what is expected of him and is able to jump by himself with good form, he will have to jump under saddle and also learn to deal with the rider's weight.

JUMPING on the LONGE LINE at SEMILIBERTY over a SINGLE OBSTACLE

It is understandable that before asking the horse to jump any kind of obstacle on the longe line, you must make certain that he will walk, trot, and canter on the flat at your slightest voice command. It would also be best if he knew how to halt, stand still, and even reverse direction.

Before you begin the work with your Gentil Helper, lay one rail across the track with a low standard at each end. Also, to facilitate the lesson in both directions, set two single rails in oblique, each resting on either side of the inside standard and parallel to the track. (See Fig. 58.) This will allow the longe line to slide over and not catch onto the standard while the horse is going over the jump.

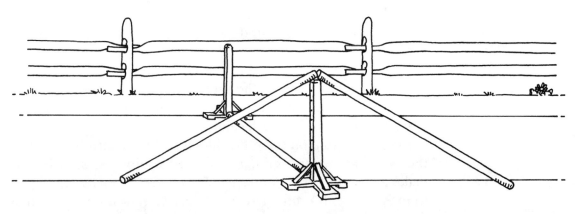

FIG. 58

The following progression will be done tracking left. (It will be the opposite tracking right.)

Fasten the longe line to a longeing cavesson, a halter, or simply through the bit if the horse has a bridle. Then, holding the line about 10 inches from his face, quietly lead him over the rail on the ground. If at first the horse is a little reluctant or frightened, do not stare at him, but by increasing the tension on the longe line, insist until he follows you. (See Fig. 59.)

• Several times walk back and forth over the rail until the horse is totally indifferent but obedient.

• Then, tracking left at the walk, longe the horse on a circle tangent to the track, directly in front of the rail.

• Progressively, move the circle closer toward the rail, until finally, with each revolution, the horse has to go over it.

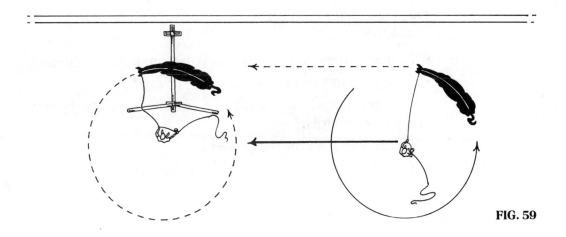

FIG. 59

The EDUCATION of the HORSE

• When the horse has understood and is totally confident, ask him to trot.

For several minutes in the same manner, longe him over the rail until he maintains a steady pace at the trot without attempting to jump in any fashion.

From this point on the procedure is simple: continue longeing the horse at the trot and, every 2 or 3 minutes, stop him to make a change between the two standards. Then ask the horse to pick up the trot on a circle and lead him again over the new construction.

Ask your Gentil Helper to make the changes as follows:

• Adding two rails, build a low crossrail about 18 inches high, leaving one rail in front as a ground pole to facilitate the takeoff.

• Progressively raise the crossrail to about 2 feet 6 inches.

• Add two low standards and one more rail to build a second crossrail standing 2 feet behind the existing one.

• Transform the second crossrail to a low vertical about 2 feet 6 inches in height.

• Transform the first crossrail to a low vertical about 2 feet high.

You will now have a ramplike oxer type of fence, which you will widen and raise as the work progresses. (See Fig. 60.)

**THIS EXERCISE WILL TEACH
THE HORSE**

• To pass in between two standards without being frightened.

• To walk and trot over a rail.

• To jump an obstacle and learn to cope with low heights and narrow widths.

• To learn to land on the proper lead.

• To hold his form longer in the air over a low, wider oxer.

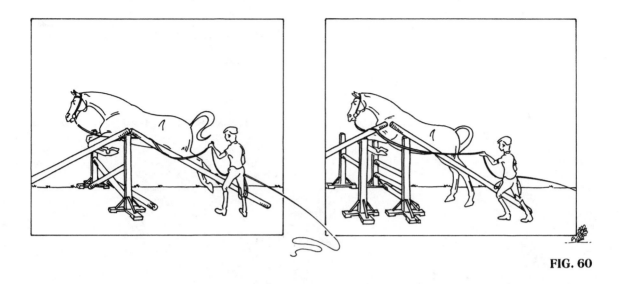

FIG. 60

HELPFUL SUGGESTIONS

Before the longeing sessions, always equip your horse with galloping, ankle, and bell boots to prevent injuries if he ungainly hits the obstacle or steps on his heels with his hind feet.

Remember, while longeing, to avoid dizziness and to keep the horse in front of you, you should CONSTANTLY focus on his hindquarters and often alter direction.

When you longe a horse over fences, you should always hold the longe whip close to his hind legs to stimulate the impulsion and to prevent a stop.

If the horse has the tendency to precipitate before the obstacle, you should set several parallel rails on the ground to hold his attention and distract him from his apprehension. The space between these rails should be about 4 feet 6 inches.

After each jumping phase, for the horse's comfort and confidence, slightly loosen the longe line to avoid pulling on his mouth.

If the horse runs out, immediately stop him with a strong tug on the longe line and simultaneously, but vigorously, rap his hind legs with the longe whip to show your discontent. Then let him think about it for a few seconds and give him a friendly pat on the neck for forgiveness. Early in the training, the horse MUST learn to go over the obstacle and not stop in front of it!

If the horse does not respect the obstacle and continues knocking it down, you may use cavalletti (a cavalletto is a rail that has small but heavy supports at each end) or solid fences such as heavy logs or railroad ties. (See Fig. 61.)

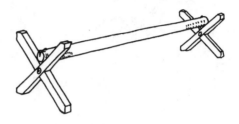

FIG. 61 Cavaletto

JUMPING on the LONGE LINE over an IN-AND-OUT COMBINATION

The goal of jumping a single obstacle is primarily to prepare the horse to learn what is expected of him. But jumping over a succession of two obstacles separated by one canter stride will teach him how to do it well and to find his own takeoff spot. In other words, the true learning experience will begin *inside* the combination.

With your Gentil Helper, lay four rails together on the track, with one standard on either end and two other rails leaning on the inside standard top for the longe line to slide on. Then pace 18 to 21 feet away (six to seven steps) and set up four other rails on the ground, with two standards side by side on either end, plus two rails in oblique for the longe line.

The following progression will be done tracking to the left. (It will be the opposite tracking to the right.)

Just as you did for the single obstacle, lead the horse back and forth over the line of rails. When he is relaxed and confident, begin longeing him on a circle tangent to the track and directly in front of the first set of rails. As soon as you have obtained the horse's attention, guide him through the line, following from an inside track. After the last element, begin another circle and then stop him to give a rewarding little pat on the neck.

Employing the same method, proceed at the trot and several times in a row let him go over the line to get used to the idea of sustaining the trot without attempting to jump. From this point on, the procedure is simple. (See Fig. 62.)

Continue longeing the horse at the trot and every 5 minutes or so interrupt the progression to build a different obstacle. Then trot several times over the new construction. Proceed very gradually, even if it is necessary to divide the progression into a few sessions. At the end, your horse will be accustomed to the routine of going over the rails and will be confident about it as well as be stabilized in his pace.

Ask your Gentil Helper to build the obstacles in the following order:

- Build a low crossrail from the second element (with the first set of standards of the second element).

- Build a low crossrail from the first element.

- Build a second crossrail with the second set of the second element.

- Transform the last crossrail to a low vertical fence about 2 feet high.

- Build a low oxer with the second element, the back rail 6 inches higher than the front.

- Transform the first element to a low vertical about 2 feet in height, with one ground rail on either side.

When the horse is able to jump the combination quietly, it will be time to teach him to use his body properly, to develop his style, and to improve his confidence.

A horse is said to jump with "good form" when, on top of the obstacle, he lowers his head, stretches his neck down, rounds his top line from his ears to his tail, equally raises his two knees, and tucks his hind legs under his body. If the horse fails to round his back and keeps his head up in the air, he will be

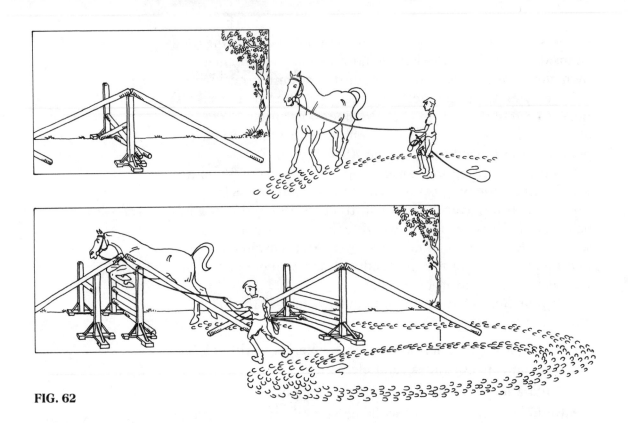

FIG. 62

considered "flat" or "hollow" and jump like a miniature French poodle.

To improve your horse's style, you will realize that:

• Jumping a vertical obstacle from a trot will teach him to engage his hindquarters, to raise his shoulders, and to bascule (round his top line) on the top of the fence.

• Jumping an oxer (of average size) will teach him to fold his front legs and to hold his form longer.

• Jumping a wide oxer will teach him to stretch and to extend his top line because he has no speed to help him raise his shoulders.

As you progress in the jumping of the combination, gradually, a few inches at a time, *shorten* the distance between the two obstacles. This will be the greatest lesson because it will teach your horse to compress, to regroup his legs (collection), and to make him curl and bascule his body over the second fence. The repeated practice will develop power in his hindquarters and give him the ability to move forward, yet still round.

Jumping the combination in reverse order, i.e., oxer to vertical, will teach him to further engage his hind legs and raise his shoulders.

The most difficult gymnastic is to ask the horse to jump the combination from a canter. To do so:

- Canter the horse on a circle, five to six strides (60 to 70 feet) away from the first element and tangent to the track.
- Lead him toward the combination, maintaining the same rhythm.
- Let him jump the line and follow him through and release the longe line.
- Reorganize the pace on a circle after the second obstacle.

It is said to be the hardest exercise because YOU will have to RUN and perhaps GALLOP along with the horse (see Fig. 63, next page).

THESE EXERCISES WILL TEACH THE HORSE

- To develop his style without the use of speed.
- To raise his shoulders and to round his back.
- To compress and extend his body.
- To improve his balance and ability to perform.
- To form the habit of landing on the proper canter lead.

HELPFUL SUGGESTIONS

Before you begin the actual work over a combination of fences, you will have to teach a new longeing exercise to your horse; he has to learn to walk, trot, or canter around you while you move the center of the circle. To do so, you will stand almost at the end of the ring, on the centerline, and proceed as follows (see Fig. 63):

A. Begin longeing the horse at the walk (later on you will repeat this exercise at the trot, and then at the canter).

B. Slowly, step-by-step, walk up and down the centerline, longeing the horse around you. Progress with caution until the horse is accustomed to seeing you in motion beside him.

C. Gradually step faster and even jog slowly.

After a few lessons, tracking in both directions, you must reach the point where you will be able to *run* on the centerline while retaining the horse at a quiet canter and following the path of the track.

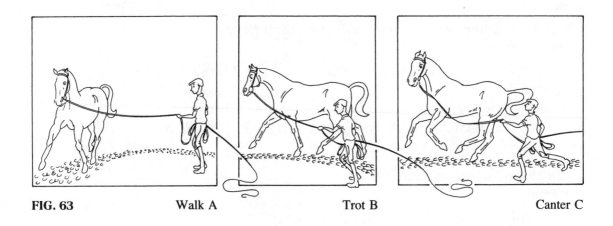

FIG. 63 Walk A Trot B Canter C

To teach the horse to adjust his stride from the top of the obstacle as opposed to the base, progressively move the ground pole from the front to directly under the obstacle, then beyond it, and, finally, remove it completely (see Fig. 64).

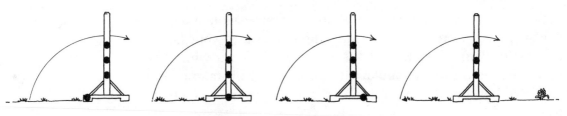

FIG. 64

The HANDBOOK of JUMPING ESSENTIALS

When the horse begins jumping the combination, if he has the tendency to rush or precipitate, you will set one rail on the ground in the middle of the distance he has to cover between the two obstacles. This will keep his attention and compel him to slow down.

If you have the opportunity to work with a perfectly trained horse on the longe line, you could ask him to jump the single obstacle from a walk, a standstill, and even from a backward motion. This will tremendously develop the power of his hind-quarters, propel his shoulders to rise higher, and allow him to use his neck and head to better bascule over the top of the obstacle.

This training procedure can also be accomplished with one longe line on each side of the horse's body to act as long-reins. It is called long-reining. The results are quicker because it is a more precise work, but it necessitates a subtle and delicate execution.

JUMPING under SADDLE

Mother Nature has provided a perfect balance for the horse, but it seems that she has forgotten to include the rider. Therefore, we have to teach the horse to cope with the rider's weight.

For best results with the following progression, your horse should have sufficient knowledge on the flat. At the walk, trot, and canter, the better he is able to sustain balance, rhythm, and impulsion, the better and the faster he will assimilate the work over fences.

Always remember the saying, "While being ridden, if a horse is not learning, he is unlearning." Knowing this, simultaneously with the study of the jumping every day, you will instill and improve the obedience to the natural aids on the flat by perfecting and furthering his education.

Teaching the Horse to Jump
a Single Obstacle at the Trot

With your Gentil Helper, set one rail on the ground across the track.

Just as you did previously, ride your horse at a walk and several times go back and forth over the rail.

Then your Gentil Helper successively will, after a couple of passages, add four rails on the ground about 4 feet and 6 inches apart. (See Fig. 65.)

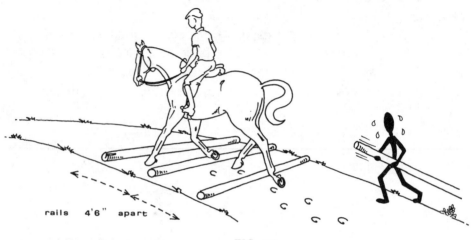

rails 4'6" apart

FIG. 65

When the horse is familiar with the rails and realizes that they "do not bite"—by this, I mean it is safe—you will proceed in the same manner, but at the posting trot. To give comfort to the horse while trotting over the rails, slightly lean your upper body more forward and barely touch the saddle with your seat on the way down.

After several attempts, your horse should quietly trot on loose reins over the rails. If not, you should start the phase over at the walk, and the next time you approach at the trot, slow the pace a few feet before the first rail.

Now ask your Gentil Helper to set two standards on either end and to regroup four rails, leaving the remaining rail about 9 feet ahead.

Track to the left (it will be the opposite tracking to the right), and proceeding at a posting trot and heading always in the same direction, go several times over the rails on the ground. It would be a wise idea, at this point, to ask the horse to always come back to a standstill a few strides after the "jump". This action will teach your horse to rebalance himself following the obstacle. It may be somewhat difficult at first, but before long, he will anticipate your command and stop almost on his own.

From this point on, the procedure is simple: every four to five trips, or at your own discretion, ask your Gentil Helper to build a different obstacle. Going from the easiest to the most difficult, it would be:

- A low crossrail about 18 inches in height with one ground pole on either side (18 inches away).
- A higher crossrail about 2 or 2½ feet high.
- A low vertical fence about 2 feet high.
- A low oxer, 2 feet high in the front, 2 feet 3 inches in the back, and 2 feet in width.

Transform the obstacle only when you are certain that the horse is jumping calmly. After each jump, do not forget to settle in a halt for a moment.

THIS EXERCISE WILL TEACH THE HORSE

- To cope with the rider's weight while jumping.
- To raise his shoulders over a vertical.
- To engage and round his spinal column over an oxer.
- To develop his confidence.

HELPFUL SUGGESTIONS

If the horse rushes or precipitates:
Away from the obstacle, begin a circle and settle the pace, or in the worst case, walk him or let him stand for a while to give him a chance to completely relax.
Nine feet in front of the obstacle, lay one rail on the ground.

Then 4½ feet apart add three rails. If, purposely, the rails are not absolutely set parallel, it will incite the horse to trot over them with more caution.

When the horse is about to take off, progressively tighten your legs without surprising him and release the tension of the reins to allow him to find his own spot.

If the horse has a tendency to jump hollow, which is a very uncomfortable attitude for the rider, loosen the reins and hold onto the mane or a neck strap. In good time, after more jumping exercises, this bad posture will be rectified.

Teaching the Horse to Jump
Several Obstacles at the Trot

With your Gentil Helper, randomly scatter all over the ring and set apart from each other, five to six single obstacles, such as: two crossrails, two verticals, and two oxers. Each obstacle will be low and have one ground pole on either side so that it will be easy to jump from either direction. (See Fig. 66.)

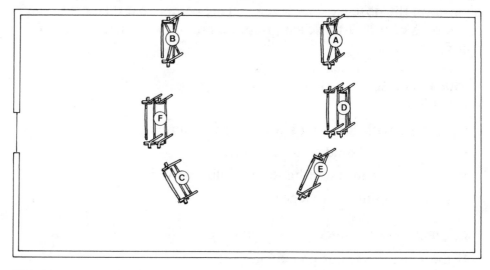

FIG. 66

For example:
Starting track to the left, trot A, canter two or three strides,

and halt your horse (halt means stand *still*). Trot B and halt again. Then proceeding in the same manner, trot C, D, E, F, and A from the opposite direction.

When your horse is stabilized, relaxed, and halts after each obstacle, try to trot a different course, such as AEDFCBA or EADBFECA, or whatever choice you have made.

While trotting the obstacles, take advantage of the flat phases in between the landing and the takeoff zones to modify the pace of your horse by alternately switching from a lengthening to a shortening to a lengthening again, or vice versa, so that your horse will learn to fix his attention on your demands instead of leaning on the bit. He also will learn to prepare himself for the next obstacle.

After jumping four to five different short courses, try to jump one more, but this time WITHOUT stopping after each obstacle. Amazingly, you will realize that following the landing phases, your horse will have a steady pace and quietly wait for your command. But it will be too soon yet to omit halting after the obstacles from the training.

When you approach the obstacles, leave the horse alone to give him a chance to figure out how to negotiate the jump. You will approach the fence as follows:

SEAT: in light contact with the saddle.

LEGS: acting together at the girth to maintain the engagement and the impulsion.

HANDS: in soft contact with the horse's mouth, but ready to act if the balance changes.

**THIS EXERCISE WILL TEACH
THE HORSE**

• To lengthen his attention span.

• To develop his confidence.

• To develop the ability to promptly re-establish his balance after a jump.

• To perfect the obedience to the rider's aids.

HELPFUL SUGGESTIONS

If your horse does not want to approach a new obstacle because he is frightened, bring him back to a walk or even a halt. Let him look at it from a distance, then try to approach it slowly. At the beginning of the learning period, horses frequently feel the need to touch or smell those strange constructions. If the horse is totally reluctant to approach the obstacle, ask him, facing the fence, to back up several times in a row and then try again. Often when you back a horse, unconsciously, you develop within his mind the desire to move forward. Incidentally, you will proceed in the same manner if, one day, you have to retrain a "stopper" (horse that has a tendency to refuse to jump).

If your horse gives you satisfaction in the progress of his studies, never hesitate to reward him with a little pat on the neck. Even better, bring him back to his stall. To him, this will be the ultimate reward.

Teaching the Horse to Jump a Single Obstacle at the Canter

With your Gentil Helper lay four rails down together on the track, with one standard on either side. Then pace 28 to 30 feet (ten to eleven steps) and repeat the same operation with four other rails and two standards.

At the walk, you will ride your horse back and forth over the rails. During the learning process, always begin with a known work before attempting a new one. Then when your horse is familiar with the exercise, proceed with the same routine at the posting trot.

After several trips, bring your horse back to a walk and ask your Gentil Helper to build a low crossrail in between the second pair of standards.

Tracking left (it will be the opposite if the setup were in reverse order), trot over the rails on the ground, and then, the crossrail. After repeating this exercise two or three times, ask your Gentil Helper to construct a second crossrail in between the first set of standards.

To go over this line, ride as follows: at a distance from the first obstacle, pick up the posting trot, establish the pace, and guide the horse toward the first element. Continuing at the trot, go over the first crossrail and give total freedom to your horse to jump the second obstacle. (Do not omit the halt afterward.) The first crossrail will incite the horse to canter, and the predetermined distance between the two obstacles will help him to canter two strides and have enough time to find a comfortable takeoff spot to jump the second crossrail.

After several trips, your Gentil Helper will transform the second element to a vertical fence about 2 feet in height and add a little coop under it. After every other trip over the combination, the second element will be raised 3 inches by 3 inches until it reaches 3 to 3½ feet high.

When you jump the second element, you will feel (see Fig. 67):

ON THE FLAT: the horse is light if he is well balanced.

BEFORE THE TAKEOFF: the horse lowering his forehand to allow the hindquarters to engage under his body.

DURING THE TAKEOFF: the horse raising his forelegs and propelling himself with his hind legs.

FIG. 67 (cont. next page)

ON TOP OF THE OBSTACLE: the horse rounding his spinal column. You may feel that your weight is being propelled upward.

DURING THE LANDING PHASE: the horse lowering his forehand to allow his hindquarters to engage and rebalance himself.

FIG. 67 (cont.)

When the horse is fully accustomed to the trotting combination, add a third element to the line: an oxer about 21 to 22 feet away or seven to eight steps. At first the oxer will be low and ramped, 2 feet high in the front, 2½ feet in the back, and 2 feet wide. Then, gradually, as you jump the combination and as the horse becomes more agile, raise the top rails 3 inches by 3 inches until it reaches 3 feet in the front, 3 feet 6 inches in the back, and 3 to 3 feet 6 inches in width.

From this point on, the procedure will be simple: after three or four trips, if you do not encounter any difficulties, you will progressively spread the distance 12 feet by 12 feet to add strides between the vertical and the oxer. (See Fig. 68.)

When the horse is able to jump the third element with ease, it will be time to eliminate the two preceding obstacles and slightly lower the oxer 3 or 6 inches all the way around.

To jump this single obstacle, proceed as follows: away from the oxer, pick up the canter on a circle. Establish the balance, the rhythm, the impulsion, and then go large (go around the

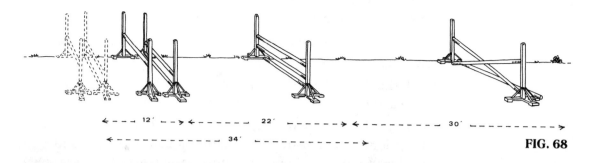

12' 22' 30'

34'

FIG. 68

ring on the track), directing the horse toward the obstacle. In the approach:

If you see a distance that is too long:

A. Focus on the base of the fence. This will incite the horse to a closer takeoff spot.

B. Or wait until you see a shorter distance.

C. Or bring the horse back to a trot, but jump the obstacle anyway.

If you do not like the distance you see, avoid pulling up because you may very well teach your horse to become a "stopper." Instead, keep him balanced and let him find a spot on his own.

If suddenly the horse changes the pace, try to make a quick and discreet adjustment. If the horse does not obey, school your horse as follows:

A. About five strides before the obstacle, slow the pace to obtain the trot (you may have to use firm hand actions, such as half-halts—see page 115).

B. Several times repeat phase A and progressively reduce the trotting strides to 4, 3, 2, 1, and none.

THESE EXERCISES WILL TEACH YOUR HORSE

• To jump at the canter.
• To improve his balance.
• To be attentive to your natural aids.
• To build his own confidence.

HELPFUL SUGGESTIONS

Here are some fundamental exercises to improve your horse's style over the fences:

• If the horse has the tendency to jump too high, simply increase the speed during the approach.

• If the horse has the tendency to be too lazy or not pay attention, either widen the oxer when it is low or add two rails set up in the shape of an upside-down **V**. (See Fig. 69.) For schooling purposes, the rails should first be lying on the ground, and when the horse is accustomed to their presence, it will be time to rest them on the top rail.

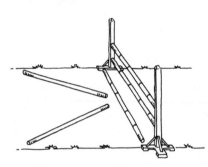

FIG. 69

• If the horse is jumping too aggressively, roll away the ground pole or shorten the distances within the lines.

• If the horse is too slow unfolding his front legs, set up a "no stride" combination, with two or more crossrails spaced only 12 feet apart. This will force the horse to "bounce," which means to quickly land and take off between the obstacles because he has not enough room to canter one full stride. (See Fig. 70.)

• If the horse has the tendency to "hang" his front legs, make him jump as many wide oxers as you can or jump combinations, such as a high vertical to a wide oxer.

• If the horse has the tendency to drift within the line, either increase the impulsion or lay rails on the ground on either side of the track to "canalize" the horse. (See Fig. 71.)

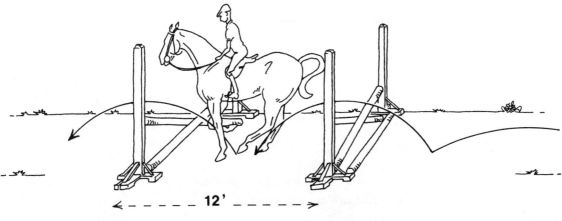

12'

FIG. 70

• If your horse still shows a certain lack of attention, school him to jump subtle mixed lines such as a low crossrail, 18 to 21 feet to a vertical, 34 feet to an oxer, 24 feet to another vertical, or a more difficult line—a low crossrail, 12 feet to another crossrail, 21 feet to an oxer, 34 feet to a vertical, 24 feet to an oxer.

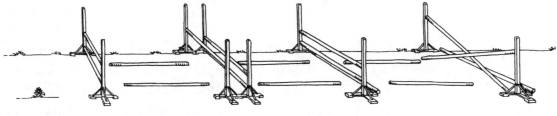

FIG. 71

Always remember to *halt* your horse after the last jump to teach him to rebalance himself. To establish the halt, use only your seat (with your upper body slightly leaning backward), your legs, and your hands. Avoid using the outside fencing or a wall for stopping, even though it helps to better engage the horse. Look at it in this manner: the fencing or the wall may not always be there when you need it.

In the progression of the training, you may encounter some

good days and some . . . different ones. But NEVER let your temper get in the way. If you feel frustrated or angry, walk your horse for a few minutes, take several deep breaths, and begin again. In the worst case, dismount and leave the horse alone until the next day—you and your horse will both feel much better then and can repair peacefully what could have led to a catastrophe.

Teaching the Horse to Lengthen and to Shorten His Strides to Meet a Spot

The horse must learn to extend and to compress his spinal column to be able to jump long and short distances between obstacles with ease. For the following study, you will jump over a two-stride combination, but it would be similar if the distances were stretched out to three, four, five, or more strides.

TO LENGTHEN THE STRIDES

With your Gentil Helper, build an in-and-out combination on the track with two low, but wide, ramped oxers and leave one ground pole on either side. The distance in between the obstacles will be at approximately 32 to 34 feet apart (ten to eleven steps).

Far from the combination, tracking left, pick up the canter on a circle. Establish the balance, the rhythm, and the impulsion. Then go large toward the first oxer and ride as follows:

A. Seek an average takeoff spot. After you have jumped the first element, let your horse negotiate the two following canter strides and meet the second obstacle without your help. The only actions that you will intend to control are the straightness and the impulsion.

B. Ask your Gentil Helper to stretch the inside distance by moving one of the two oxers farther back by about 1 foot to stretch the distance to 33 to 35 feet.

Then establish the canter, the balance, etc. . . . Look for an average spot but this time, when you land after the first obstacle, act a little stronger with your legs to help the horse to cover the new distance of which he is not aware.

C. Again, stretch the spacing to 34 to 36 feet and execute the same work, acting stronger with your legs.

The repeated exercises, tracking left as well as right, will develop the ability to lengthen the horse's strides at your slightest demand.

You also may vary the exercises by lowering the first oxer to reduce the jumping arc to incite the horse to lengthen the canter strides in between the obstacles.

TO SHORTEN THE STRIDES

Now build two vertical obstacles on the track without ground poles about 3 to 3 feet 3 inches high and spaced 32 to 34 feet apart (ten to eleven steps).

Away from the combination, tracking left, pick up the canter and immediately establish the balance, the rhythm, and the impulsion. Then you will go large toward the first vertical and ride as follows:

A. As you are approaching the first element, lengthen the strides, holding your reins adjusted, and look for a long takeoff spot. After you have landed on the other side, ride more aggressively with your legs at the girth, but this time with looser reins to take off from a closer spot. A tight spot will only encourage your horse to compress his body, to collect his legs, and to curl on the top of the second obstacle.

B. Now shorten the distance between the two verticals to 31 or 33 feet and proceed in the same manner. But this time, remain more *passive* with your leg actions and steady the pace with your hands. Let the horse learn the lesson to collect himself.

C. Shorten the distance to 30 or 32 feet. As you ride the line, your hand actions will be somewhat identical, yet softer.

The repeated exercises, tracking left as well as right, will develop the ability to shorten the horse's strides at your slightest demand.

You also may vary the exercises by widening the first oxer to increase the jumping arc to incite the horse to shorten the canter strides in between the obstacles.

It would be a wise idea to combine these two exercises by building one long and one short combination on each long side of the ring. (See Fig 72.) At your own discretion, go back and forth over these two lines. Also, you will realize that it is easier to lengthen than to shorten the strides because horses prefer to move on rather than to slow down.

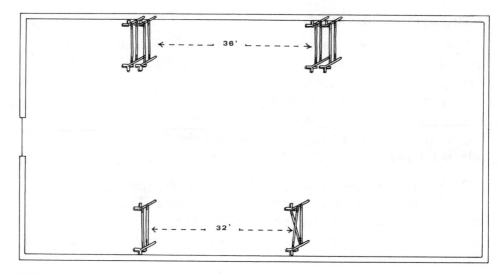

FIG. 72

THESE EXERCISES WILL TEACH YOUR HORSE

- To stretch his body and yet still stay round.
- To compress his body and to perfect the engagement of his hind legs.
- To easily switch from a long position to a short one.
- To improve his balance.
- To perfect the obedience to your aid demands.

As you progress, your aid actions must be more precise, but NEVER simultaneous. Remember:

- When your legs act—your hands do not but may resist.
- When your hands act—your legs do not but may resist.

As your coordination of the aids improve, your actions will occur closer together, but NEVER at the same time. Leave this subtlety to experts or artist riders, because it could only confuse your inexperienced horse.

The promptness of the obedience to your leg and hand actions is a MUST. You should know exactly how long a time your horse will take before he responds to your demands.

Your legs must act *stronger*, but *not faster*, to avoid the precipitation of the gait and also to avoid interfering with the rhythm.

With time and practice, you will lessen the usage of your voice aid and learn to converse with your horse by using your legs and your hands.

- When you tighten your legs, you are in fact saying, "Go forward and bring your hindquarters under your body."
- When you tighten your fingers on the reins, you are saying, "Slow down or turn, but stay balanced."

The conversation with your horse should be a private matter. . . .

With time and practice, your aid actions must become more discreet and softer: your horse has to learn to jump with very little help from you. If you acquire the habit of adjusting too much, soon your horse will depend completely upon you and no longer try on his own.

If the horse does not compress well or is a slow learner, add a ground pole 1 or 2 feet in front of the second obstacle to remind him to shorten his strides.

Once your horse has gained sufficient flexibility to lengthen and to shorten his strides, it will be time to repeat the above exercises, jumping lines with 3, 4, 5, 6, and even 7 strides in between the two obstacles.

Teaching the Horse
to Jump a Double
and a Triple Combination

A double or a triple combination is a "skill test" for both the horse and the rider, but in reality, it is easy to jump. The only challenge consists of negotiating the approach to the first element correctly.

THE DOUBLE COMBINATION
(FOR HUNTER, EQUITATION,
AND JUMPERS)

A double combination consists of two consecutive obstacles with one or two strides in between each element. The entire in-and-out setup is considered as being one fence.

On the track, lay down two sets of three to four rails and four standards, spaced about 22 to 24 feet apart eight steps. (See Fig. 73.) In this study, to be absolutely precise, you should "tape measure" the distance from the top of each obstacle. For an oxer, the top is situated in the middle between the two highest rails.

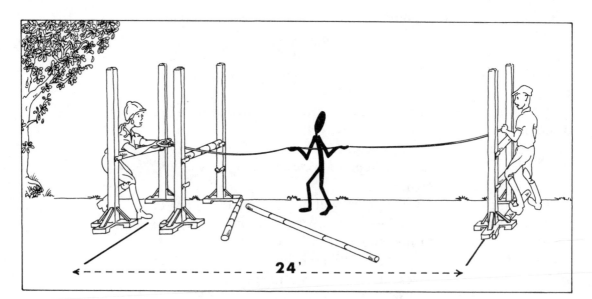

FIG. 73

To predispose your horse, begin by riding over the rails at the walk and at the trot. Then build one crossrail in between each set of standards. Several times canter quietly back and forth over the combination. Finally, raise the obstacle to about 3 to 3½ feet high.

Away from the combination, tracking left, pick up the canter on a circle, establish the balance, the rhythm, and the impulsion. Then go large and proceed in your approach according to the different types of combinations as the following chart indicates:

FIG. 74

Double combination with one average stride (24 feet)

	Obstacle	Pace	Spot	Legs	Hands
vertical-vertical	first	forward	long	active	resist
	second	forward	long	active	resist
vertical-oxer	first	forward	long	active	resist
	second	normal	short	passive	yield
oxer-oxer	first	normal	short	passive	yield
	second	normal	short	passive	yield
 oxer-vertical	first	normal	short	passive	yield
	second	forward	long	active	resist

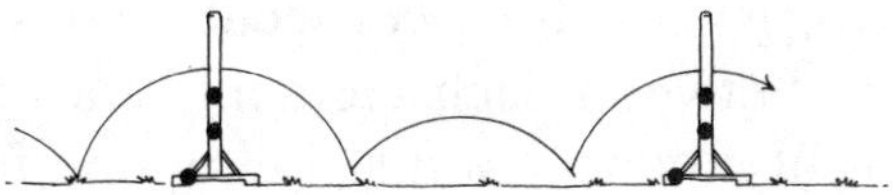

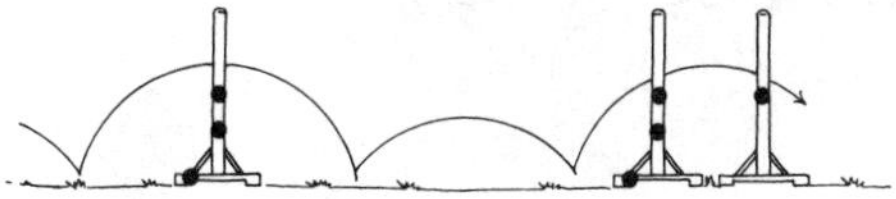

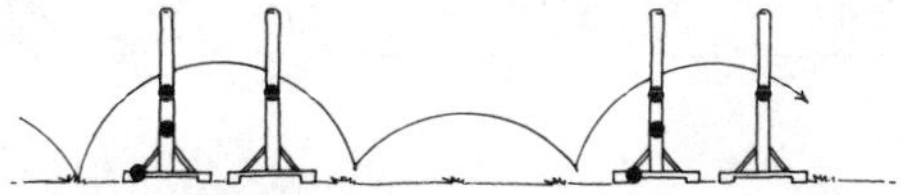

The procedure will be identical to jump a two-stride in-and-out combination. However:

• If the distance between the two obstacles is longer than 36 feet, you will have to approach the combination with a longer stride, be more aggressive with your legs, and increase the contact with the horse's mouth to incite him to take off sooner.

• If the distance is less than 36 feet, you will have to approach with a shorter stride, preserve the impulsion with your legs, and steady the pace with a resisting hand action all through the combination. Then ride the two obstacles as described in the chart.

THE TRIPLE COMBINATION
(FOR EQUITATION AND JUMPERS ONLY)

A triple combination consists of three consecutive obstacles with one or two strides in between each element, and in any order. The entire setup is also considered as being one fence.

Now add a third element to the existing combination. To do so, measure 34 to 36 feet and build a new obstacle with four to six rails and four standards. (See Fig. 75.)

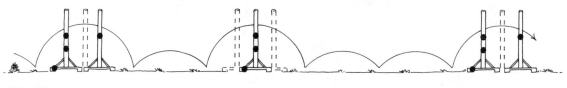

FIG. 75

At a good distance away from the triple combination, tracking right, pick up the canter on a circle, establish the balance, the rhythm, and the impulsion. Then go large to jump the line and adjust your approach according to the different types of obstacles as the following chart indicates:

	Obstacle	Pace	Spot	Legs	Hands
	first	forward	long	active	resist
	second	forward	long	active	resist
vertical-vertical-vertical	third	forward	long	active	resist
	first	forward	long	active	resist
	second	forward	long	active	resist
vertical-vertical-oxer	third	normal	short	passive	yield
	first	forward	long	active	resist
	second	normal	short	passive	yield
vertical-oxer-oxer	third	normal	short	passive	yield
	first	forward	long	active	resist
	second	normal	short	passive	yield
vertical-oxer-vertical	third	forward	long	active	resist
	first	normal	short	passive	yield
	second	normal	short	passive	yield
oxer-oxer-oxer	third	normal	short	passive	yield
	first	normal	short	passive	yield
	second	normal	short	passive	yield
oxer-oxer-vertical	third	forward	long	active	resist
	first	normal	short	passive	yield
	second	forward	long	active	resist
oxer-vertical-vertical	third	forward	long	active	resist
	first	normal	short	passive	yield
	second	forward	long	active	resist
oxer-vertical-oxer	third	normal	short	passive	yield

Complications will occur in a triple combination if one of the distances requires a lengthening or shortening of the strides. Always bear in mind that what is good for the first and the second obstacle may not be necessarily the same for the third. Also, be aware of the fact that your horse may make an inappropriate error.

Before attempting to jump such a combination, make certain that you know the exact distances in between the fences and remember this fundamental rule:

"To minimize the adjustments in a triple combination, the rider MUST concentrate on the second element."

In other words, if the distance between the two first elements is short, you should approach the first and the second obstacle rather quietly but avoid shortening the strides too much so that you are still able to cover the second distance. If the distance between the two first elements is long, you should approach the first and the second obstacle with more forward motion but avoid lengthening too much so that you still have enough room for the second distance.

THESE EXERCISES WILL TEACH YOUR HORSE

- To perfect his abilities to jump.
- To be more flexible in adjusting his strides.
- To be more attentive to your aids.
- To jump any type of course.

HELPFUL SUGGESTIONS

During the progress of the schooling sessions, to shorten the spacing between two obstacles, you also may raise the vertical, widen the oxer inward, or simply roll away the ground pole.

Avoid trying to help your horse off the ground by standing on your stirrup irons, as you will only disturb his balance. Instead, allow him to make the final decision of when to take off. Once the horse is in the air, release the rein contact. Do not forget to give him all the freedom he may need to stretch his top line.

Teaching the Horse to Turn
on Top of an Obstacle

In a jumping course, obstacles can be positioned at each extremity of a bending line and sometimes in the middle of the turns. The tightness of these turns will be in direct relation to the type of course to be jumped.

PREPARATION ON THE FLAT

Teach your horse to turn at your slightest indication. To do so:

A. In the ring, preserving straightness and the horse's balance, canter down the centerline on the left lead. Three strides away from the end, look to your left (it will be the opposite for a right turn) and then, moving your right arm slightly forward, *loosen the right rein*. This *release* will increase the tension of the left rein and compel the horse to turn left.

Several times, execute the same exercise, alternating left lead–left turn and right lead–right turn. (See Fig. 76.)

To Turn:
RELEASE

FIG. 76

The EDUCATION of the HORSE   97

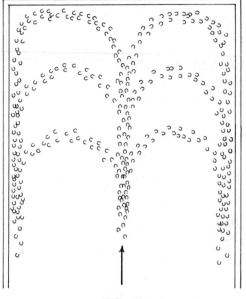

FIG. 77

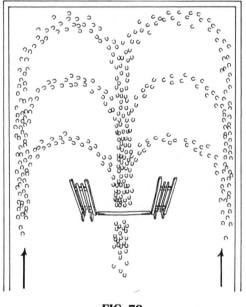

FIG. 78

B. Proceed in the same manner but gradually turn, six, nine, or more strides before reaching the end of the center-line.

C. Reverse the process: tracking left, canter along the long side of the ring; three strides before the end, look to your left and progressively release the right rein to allow the horse to come up the centerline.

Several times, execute the same exercise tracking left and right.

D. About 70 feet from the short side of the ring, lay down one rail across the centerline with a standard on either end. Tracking left (it will be the opposite tracking right), canter down the long side and, three strides before the end of the ring, turn your head to the left and look at the ground pole. Then release the right rein to negotiate the turn. Remember, you must always aim for the center of the rail.

Practice several times and gradually turn sooner.

BENDING LINES

A bending line is usually a curve within the space of two obstacles placed at a 90-degree angle.

Halfway down the length of the ring and 20 feet on the inside, build a low vertical obstacle perpendicular to the track. Then following the pattern of a wide quarter of a circle, pace 70 feet toward the center of the ring to set up another low vertical parallel to the long side. (See Fig. 79.)

On the circle, pick up the left lead canter, establish the balance, the rhythm, the impulsion, and then go large.

While cantering along the track, look for the bending line and decide what option you will take, knowing that you have basically three choices:

Option 1—The normal route.

Meeting each obstacle straight at its center will give you a smooth turn with five easy strides.

Option 2—The short route.

Meeting each obstacle at an angle will give you a straight line with four forward strides in between.

Option 3—The long route.

Meeting the first obstacle almost straight and the second at a slight angle will allow you to add one or two more strides.

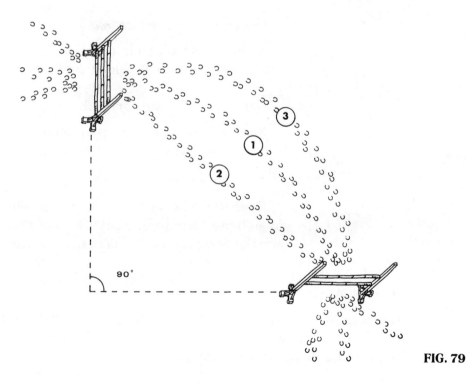

90°

FIG. 79

In your progression, practice riding bending lines with various stridings in between as well as turning left and right.

THE TURNS

With your Gentil Helper, build a single low vertical obstacle in the middle of the ring, perpendicular to the centerline.

Tracking left, pick up the canter, establish the balance, the rhythm, the impulsion, and then go large.

Turns before the obstacle.

Canter the long side of the ring, and as soon as you pass the side of the obstacle, look at it and decide which way to turn, knowing that a turn gives you three choices (see Fig. 80):

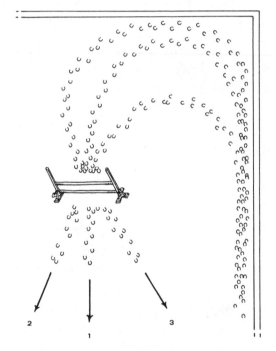

Option 1—The normal approach.

Meeting the obstacle straight on gives you the opportunity to see an average take-off spot.

Option 2—The short approach.

Meeting the obstacle at an angle from left to right gives you a long spot.

Option 3—The long approach.

Meeting the obstacle at an angle from right to left gives you more time to see a spot.

Remember: always look where you want to go before attempting any turn and then aim the horse for the center of the obstacle.

FIG. 80

Turns in the air

Approach the obstacle straight, sustaining a well-balanced canter. Look for an average spot and proceed as follows:
Look in the direction you wish to turn.

WAIT until your horse has left the ground and then apply the aids:

SEAT: shift your weight to the inside stirrup iron, i.e., left stirrup for a left-hand turn.

LEGS: the inside leg acts at the girth to maintain the impulsion; the outside leg, behind the girth, is ready to resist to prevent the haunches from drifting to the outside.

HANDS: the inside hand acts with a leading rein (see appendix, Rein Effect I) to indicate the direction; the outside hand yields to allow and then to regulate the turn.

The first time you turn in the air, do not turn too tight. With practice, you will be able to be more exigent and make sharper curves.

Turns after the obstacle

As your horse lands after the obstacle, promptly, but smoothly, raise your upper body to rebalance him and apply the same aids described above.

When the pattern of a jumping course calls for tight turns, simply combine the techniques of turning before the obstacle, in the air, and after the landing.

THESE EXERCISES WILL TEACH YOUR HORSE

- To improve and perfect his balance.
- To improve and perfect the obedience to your aids.
- To save time while jumping a course.
- To land on the proper lead.

HELPFUL SUGGESTIONS

Always aim for the center of an obstacle. If you err, it is most likely because you were not attentive, or you simply looked too late. Where you are looking will have a great influence on the horse; if you look to the left, he most likely will go left, and vice versa.

When you see a distance that may be suitable for your purpose, make your turn, but if your horse is a little keen, try to avoid the short approach—it could only encourage him to cut in more.

Beware of the fact that when a horse is jumping at an angle, often he will choose a longer spot and jump higher than normal.

Whatever choice you have decided upon for the turn, make sure that your horse will always follow the chosen path:

- If your horse falls into the turn, support him with a more active inside leg and an inside indirect rein (see appendix, Rein Effect III).

- If your horse drifts toward the outside of the turn, support him with a more active leg behind the girth and a firm outside indirect rein (see appendix, Rein Effect III).

But to be successful under any of these circumstances, your actions should be preceded by a stronger leg to improve the necessary engagement.

Teaching Your Horse to Jump Courses

From the preceding studies, you already have taught your horse how to jump verticals, oxers, and various types of combinations. The time has come to expand his knowledge and to familiarize him with simple courses. You shall progress gradually and in the process introduce a wide variety of new obstacles.

To teach your horse to jump an entire course, proceed as follows:

Jumping a Low Course at the Trot

Set up a simple course with low verticals, oxers, and solid obstacles (logs and chicken coops) around the track as well as on the diagonals of the ring. (See Fig. 81.)

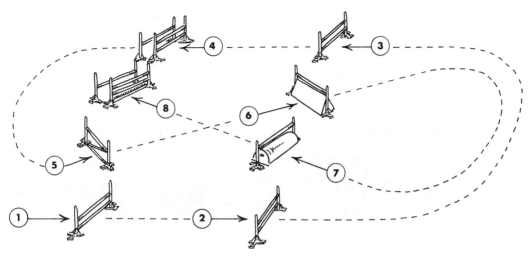

FIG. 81 Proposed course

At the trot, jump the obstacles quietly, following the pattern of one straight line after another in any order you choose. Make certain that the trot is re-established as soon as you have landed after jumping each individual obstacle. If for any reason the horse is a little impatient, make him halt after every jump; let him relax, drop the reins and, with a little pat on the neck, say to him sweetly, "Take your time, my good friend." As the horse's attitude improves, jump two successive obstacles, trot in between, and halt again. Then jump three in a row, etc. Continue increasing the number of obstacles until your horse is able to jump the entire course at a steady pace, rebalancing himself after each element.

Jumping a Low Course at the Canter

Proceed in the same manner that you did for the trot but vary the study by cantering on a circle before every obstacle. Then jump over it and begin another circle after the obstacle to still maintain the horse's balance. (See Fig. 82.) Then, beginning again, progressively add another obstacle between the circles, add two obstacles, etc. . . . .

The EDUCATION of the HORSE   103

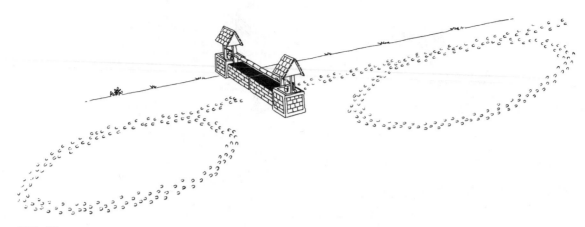

FIG. 82

When your horse is accustomed to this new type of work and is stabilized in his pace, it will be time to add one combination, more turns, bending lines, and irregular distances.

GENERAL IDEAS about VARIOUS TYPES of COURSES

Hunter Courses

A hunter course usually consists of four consecutive lines with carefully spaced obstacles on the path (shape of a figure eight). (See Fig. 83.)

To build such a course, you will use only obstacles that have a natural look, as if they were brought from a hunting field, such as posts and rails, pasture gates, brushes, logs, stone walls, chicken coops, etc. . . . Ideally, to jump such a course, the horse should sustain an even pace throughout the entire course and meet each obstacle at the correct takeoff spot to realize a perfect arc over the fence. The preselected number of strides with lines are to be respected, but a short-strided horse that cannot fulfill this contract should be compensated by sustaining a very flowing locomotion and good balance.

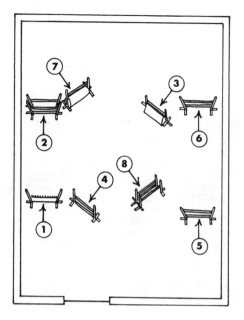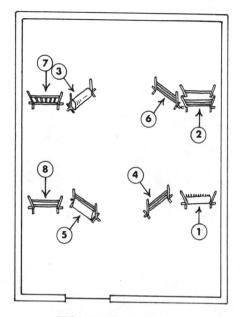

FIG. 83 Typical hunter courses

Equitation Courses

An equitation course pattern will also look like a butterfly shape (commonly known as a figure eight). Nevertheless, the turns can be tighter, and the distances unevenly spaced. (See Fig. 84, next page.)

To set up such a course, you will use obstacles from the hunting field as well as a wide variety of rails, planks, and panels painted with bright colors.

Even though only the rider should be judged in equitation classes, the course's requirements are similar to the hunter type, except that they provide a more challenging test for the horse and rider teams. In addition to the constant picture of elegance and ease that the rider will have to demonstrate during the entire course, the horse will have to cope with awkward distances, bending lines, at least one in-and-out combination, including an oxer, and two changes of canter lead, while always sustaining a proper balance and a pace suitable to the size of the obstacles.

The EDUCATION of the HORSE 105

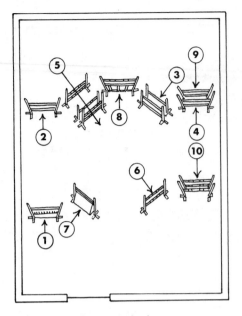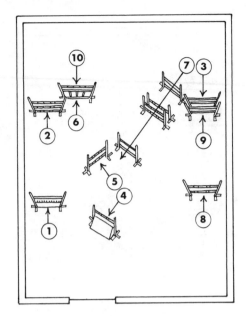

FIG. 84 Typical equitation courses

Jumper Courses

Jumper courses have unlimited varieties of patterns that are the choice of course designers in accordance with the level of the competition. Jumper courses also include a starting and finishing line that the rider must cross, in most cases, within a time limit. The jump off, also called *barrage*, is a shorter course often raised and widened to determine the winning rider.

To build such a course, you will use an even wider variety of obstacles of any look and shape providing they are safe to jump. With rails and planks, you may construct various types of verticals and spreads, such as oxers of any shape, combinations with two, three or more elements, and obstacles such as banks, triple bars, liverpools, and water jumps.

A *bank* is an amount of dirt usually covered with grass. It should be jumped with a similar approach to that of a vertical obstacle, but from a slightly closer takeoff spot to incite the horse to raise his shoulders as he will have limited room to rebalance himself on top of the obstacle. A *table bank* has a vertical takeoff and landing side and usually has three strides

The HANDBOOK of JUMPING ESSENTIALS

on top. A *derby bank* has a slope on the takeoff side and a steep downside. (See Fig. 85.)

Derby Bank

Table Bank

FIG. 85

A *triple bar*, also called spa, consists of three or more rails set up as a ramped slant and should be jumped the same as an oxer type of obstacle.

A *liverpool* is a small water hole topped with rails.

A *water jump* is a shallow ditch filled with water, at least 6 to 12 inches deep and 16 feet wide by 14 feet in spread, preceded by a small brush element no higher than 2 feet 6 inches that is placed on the takeoff side but not considered as being part of the obstacle. It should be jumped employing a similar approach to that of an oxer, but with a little more pace for the *three* last strides. During the approach, slightly loosen the reins to allow the horse to look and decide where the most appropriate place is to leave the ground.

In consideration of the horse's confidence, teach him to jump all these obstacles, beginning with low heights and shallow depths before jumping obstacles of greater heights and depths and at faster speeds. (See Fig. 86.)

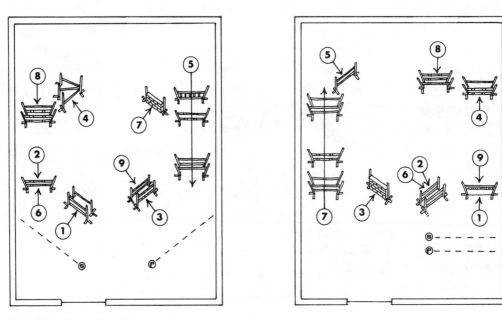

FIG. 86 Examples of jumper courses

THESE EXERCISES WILL TEACH YOUR HORSE

- To sustain various changes of pace between the fences.
- To extend his attention span and develop his confidence.
- To improve and perfect his obedience to your aids.
- To prepare him for horse shows.

HELPFUL SUGGESTIONS

Study the horse's pace. Around a small course, a horse should canter about 350 meters per minute. In a bigger area, the speed will increase to 400 and even 450 meters per minute. To learn and to feel the velocity at 350 meters per minute, proceed as follows:

• Measure the perimeter of your riding ring, remembering that 1 human step = 3 feet = 1 yard = approximately 1 meter. (One meter actually equals 1.0936 yards, but for our purposes, we shall use only a rounded figure.)

• Set a visible marker, such as a plastic cone or a low standard, where you begin measuring. Pace 525 feet and set a second marker to indicate the halfway point. Then pace another 525 feet, placing a third marker to indicate 1050 feet.

• Pick up the canter away from the starting line and establish an average pace. Then go large around the ring.

• Wearing a stopwatch, start the chronometer when you pass the first marker.

• At the halfway point, check the time, and if you have not yet reached 30 seconds, decrease the pace. If you have passed this time, increase the pace. If you are within the time, hold the same exact pace.

• At the third marker, check your watch again to see whether you went too slow or too fast or if you were within the minute accorded.

After practicing this exercise a few times, you will easily be able to feel and to maintain the 350 meter per minute rate of speed.

Proceed in the same manner for 400 and 450 meters per minute.

Measure your horse's strides. Distances between fences are based on a horse's having an average stride of 12 feet. Hence, a horse with a shorter or longer stride will find these normal distances between obstacles to be rather difficult. Before jumping a course, you should know the length of your horse's stride to make the appropriate adjustments. To do so:

• Rake a 60-foot area along the track of your riding ring.

• Confirm the 350 meter per minute pace and canter over the raked area. Then tape measure two or three strides to find the average length.

• Proceed in the same manner at the 400 and 450 meter per minute rate.

Walking a jumping course. It is important to walk a course to have a precise notion of how the obstacles look, if they have ground poles or not, if the rails rest properly in the cups, etc., and especially to measure the spacing between the obstacles.

At home, you should use a measuring tape and take the necessary time to learn how to accurately pace 24, 36, 48 feet or longer distances.

Most important to know is the exact spacing between two obstacles and to relate it to the length of your horse's stride. For example, if you pace eight steps within a one-stride in-and-out combination, this will tell you that the striding is normal. But if you pace 7½ or 8½ steps, you will know that it indicates a short or long stride, respectively.

To be precise while walking the course, you should pace the distance between two obstacles from the base on the landing side to the base of the takeoff side. (Be sure to account for half of a spread fence as part of the total measurement, otherwise your calculation will be wrong, and you may land in the oxer!) For short turns, such as bending lines, you will have to make believe that there is an imaginary line and pace the path you have chosen.

TEACHING and IMPROVING the HORSE'S FLAT WORK

To steadily progress with the horse's education, it is *most important to always mix flat work with jumping* exercises. Planning a training schedule for the month ahead is most important and will certainly facilitate the daily study of your progression. (See Fig. 87.) Also, always bear in mind that the horse's attention span is rather limited. To obtain better results with the training and to preserve the horse's willingness to work, the daily sessions should be divided into several (three or four) brief parts (about 10 minutes each) as opposed to long, tedious lessons given only once or twice a week.

MARCH

S	M	T	W	T	F	S	Notes
28 Ursula	**29**	**1** Michel S. Counter Canter Shoulder in + out. ✗	**2** Jump lines with verticals. ✗	**3** Turn out all day. ✗	**4** Bader longe over in + out. ✗	**5** Simple changes of lead. ✗	needs more work over oxers. ✗
6 longe over in + out. ✗	**7** Fanta W. Changes of lead. ✗	**8** Jump over in + out with one oxer. ✗	**9** Canter 5' each way. ✗	**10** Turn out all day. ✗	**11** flying change of lead. ✗	**12** Jump course at the trot ✗	late behind in the change of lead. ✗
13 lateral walk Canter-Canter ✗	**14** longe over oxers. ✗	**15** Flying changes. ✗	**16** John W. Canter 10' each way. Trail ride ✗	**17** Turn out 5 hours only. ✗	**18** Jump courses at the trot ✗	**19** longe on the Flat and Hack ✗	needs more work on the Flat. ✗
20 lateral work flying change of lead. ✗	**21** longe over oxers. ✗	**22** flying changes. ✗	**23** Canter 10' each way Trail ride ✗	**24** Henri Turn out all day. ✗	**25** longe 10' Flat work ✗	**26** Jump an entire horse ✗	needs to Jump more. increase feed. ✗
27 longe over in + out Ride Flat ✗	**28** Jump a course at the Canter ✗	**29** Flying changes. trot oxers ✗	**30** Canter each way. Trail ride. ✗	**31** Cris C. Turn out all day. ✗	**1**	**2**	

FIG. 87

Flat Work on the Longe Line

The longe line work on the flat is often used to release the extra energy a horse may have. But sessions that are carelessly executed or too long will only increase the horse's foolishness, and his difficulties.

Calmness, balance, straightness, and engagement should be the basic goals. Once on the longe line, the horse has to learn to wait for your demands. With a tight longeing cavesson handled *à propos*, you will easily teach him obedience and progress rapidly.

While trotting on the longe line, your first concern should be the engagement of the hind legs; the horse's hind feet must cover the footprints left by the front feet or go beyond them, but never behind. (See Fig. 88.)

To obtain this engagement, stimulate the gait with the help of a longe whip applied against the hindquarters. After several

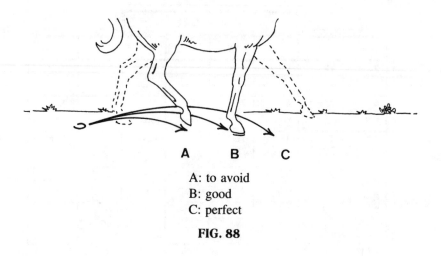

A: to avoid
B: good
C: perfect

FIG. 88

sessions, the horse will be able to stretch his hind legs and yet still slow the pace while sustaining balance and rhythm.

For horses with a weak top line or with an "upside-down" conformation, a wonderful piece of equipment was invented by Monsieur de Gogue between the two world wars. Known as the "*gogue*," it is a variable triangular system of strings going from the chest to the poll through the bit and back to the chest. This subtle tack, without harming the horse in any way, will instantaneously round his back and promote general body relaxation. The principle is simple: the pressure exerted on the horse's neck (the poll) will induce the lowering of the head, stretch the top line, and compel the engagement of the hind legs. (See Fig. 89.)

At the beginning when you first equip your horse with the gogue, it should be used only for a short amount of time. Then, progressively, you may lengthen the sessions to better develop the horse's musculature without strain. This so-called artificial aid can also be utilized while riding on the flat and over fences.

Gaits and Transitions

To be smooth and easy to obtain, the gaits and the transitions must be constantly repeated until they become comfortable for the horse to execute. The steadiness or rhythm will occur if

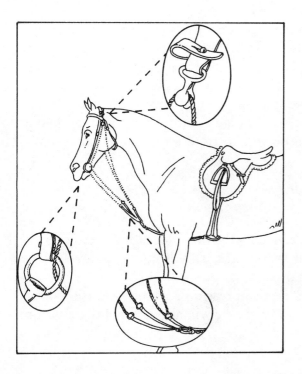

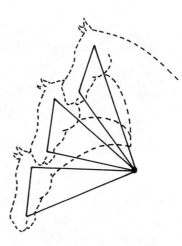

Variable triangular system

FIG. 89

you maintain the gaits for a determined period of time. For example: if you canter 5 minutes without interruption, and if you count the strides every time the horse's leading foreleg reaches the ground, soon he will settle down and relax. But at first be *very patient* and bear with the tribulations you may sometimes encounter. If there is a speed problem, you must first relax yourself by thinking positively and taking several slow deep breaths. Then begin a series of decreasing circles until you have obtained satisfaction. But in any case, retain the gait. It will be similar for the trot and walk.

The transitions must be well established, prompt and yet smooth. Their repeated demand at the same place will facilitate the learning process by taking advantage of the horse's tremendous memory until he anticipates too much.

The horse has to learn to halt perfectly at your slightest command. To do so, begin by asking for a halt from a slow walk, slightly leaning your upper body backward and sitting deeper in the saddle. Then while retaining the engagement with a steady pressure of your lower legs, ask for the halt by resisting with your hands on the reins. With practice and repetition as improvement shows, lessen your leg and hand actions and replace them with the shifting of your upper body only. If your horse has a tendency to halt crookedly, apply a preventive, but discreet, leg action behind the girth on the side he may swing.

The procedure will be similar from a trot and a canter.

The Lengthening and the Shortening of the Strides

On the flat it is imperative for the horse to learn the lengthening and the shortening of the strides. It will not only develop the flexibility of his spinal column, but will also improve the engagement. The repeated compression and the extension of his body at the walk, trot, and canter will also compel the absolute obedience to your aids.

The Lateral Movements

The lateral movements, best executed using spurs, will improve the flexibility of the joints, supple and condition the muscle system of the forehand and the hindquarters. These exercises will also develop engagement and improve the head carriage as well as create the lightness.

The lateral flexions will eliminate the muscle contractions in the neck and jaws. The direct flexions (leading to adequate head positioning for any type of work) will incite good balance and engagement. But always bear in mind that proper head carriage alone is not evidence that the horse is on the bit. To be on the bit, the horse has to have proper head carriage and be attentive to the rider's aids (see *The Handbook of Riding Essentials*).

The counter-canter and the flying change of lead are also important to maintain steadiness in the rhythm and provide balance in the turns that will bring harmony in performing the course.

To change leads, the horse must simultaneously switch his four legs. The most appropriate moment for him to do so is during the fourth phase of the canter when all his feet are off the ground. To perform a correct flying change of lead, you will apply your aids a little before the suspension phase, i.e., during the third phase when only one of the horse's four feet is on the ground. (See *The Handbook of Riding Essentials.*)

**THESE FLAT WORK EXERCISES
WILL TEACH THE HORSE**

• Obedience to the aids.

• Balance, engagement, rhythm.

• Elasticity and smoothness of the gaits.

• Freedom of the neck, proper head carriage with the mouth always lower than the rider's hands.

HELPFUL SUGGESTIONS

Sometimes while riding on the flat or over fences, check your horse and make certain by lengthening and shortening the stride that the pace and the impulsion still exist.

If, for one reason or another, when you apply the aids, nothing happens, you must think that your actions were too weak, your timing was poor, you used the improper aids, or the horse was not attentive.

The Half-Halt

The primary purpose of the half-halt is to rebalance a horse that has excessive weight on his forehand. This half-halt is a quick, yet discreet action executed with one or two hands, as follows:

1. Rotate the wrist, fingernails facing up.

2. Quickly and firmly elevate the hand (2 to 3 inches only).

These steps must be preceded by a leg action and an adjustment of the reins to avoid awkward jerks on the horse's mouth.

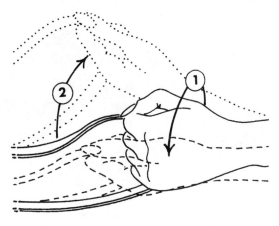

FIG. 90

For better results, the half-halt should be demanded when the horse is about to engage the hind legs, i.e., at the canter it will be between the third and fourth phase.

The other purposes of the half-halt are:

- To slow the pace.
- To shorten the strides.
- To avoid knocking a rail down with the forelegs.

If a horse left the ground from a short takeoff spot, but from a long stride, to avoid touching or knocking down the top rail, the rider will apply a tactful half-halt "in the air" to raise the horse's shoulders higher. But this action requires delicate execution and necessitates an immediate release of the reins to allow the horse to bascule on top of the obstacle.

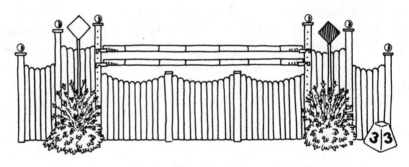

FIG. 91 Vertical picket fence with rails

CONCLUDING REMARKS

The purpose of writing these pages was to explain how to bring a horse to the best possible takeoff spot to give him the opportunity to jump round with minimum effort.

An educated rider is looking neither for a long nor a short takeoff spot, but for the most appropriate one for his or her horse's pace and the type of obstacle to jump.

As you approach an obstacle, you must make *certain* that your own body position is correct and your weight is mostly in your heels. You also have to make sure that your horse is properly balanced and on the bit with his mouth always lower than your hands.

To jump an obstacle with ease, you must be able to:

• Evaluate the distance between your horse and the best takeoff spot from as far away as possible.

• Decide whether or not you should adjust your horse's stride to reach the spot box area.

• Know what the correct adjustment should be and how to attain it.

When you see a takeoff spot, if you are not satisfied—if you feel that it is too long or you sense any doubts—WAIT one more stride and look again. You will most likely see a better one.

When it is time to make a decision, if you have not studied this book or if you are not sure whether to lengthen or shorten the strides, do NEITHER. Let your horse find his own spot, but concentrate on the most important elements—

BALANCE, RHYTHM, AND IMPULSION.

APPENDIX: The FIVE REIN EFFECTS as DESCRIBED in The HANDBOOK of RIDING ESSENTIALS by the SAME AUTHOR

The instructions for the five rein actions are given for the right rein. It would be the opposite for the left.

A hand that affects the equilibrium or the impulsion of the horse is called an active hand. A passive hand preserves the contact with the horse's mouth but does not oppose either the horse's impulsion or the active hand.

A leg that creates the impulsion or the engagement or modifies the position of the hindquarters is called an active leg. A passive leg maintains the impulsion by applying lighter contact than the active leg, without opposing it.

I	II	III
Direct Rein (Leading or Opening Rein)	**Direct Rein** of Opposition	**Indirect Rein** (Western, Supporting Bearing, and Neck Rein)

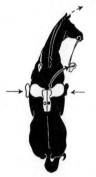 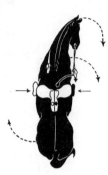 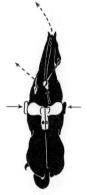

I	II	III
Right hand: Active, rotates at the wrist, fingernails facing up. The movement of the hand is forward and to the right; the elbow remains in the hip area.	Active, moves a few inches to the right and gives a parallel tension to the rear.	Active, rotates at the wrist, fingernails facing up for more strength; moves forward and slightly to the left on the neck.
Left hand: Passive, goes forward and down to yield, to allow, and then to regulate the action of the right hand.	Passive, goes forward and down to yield, to allow, and then to regulate the action of the right hand.	Passive, goes forward and down to yield, to allow, and then to regulate the action of the right hand.
Right leg: Active at the girth, slightly more forward than normal for bending.	Active at the girth, slightly stronger than the left.	Active at the girth, slightly stronger than the left, to forbid the haunches from drifting to the right.
Left leg: Active at the girth to maintain the impulsion.	Active at the girth to maintain the impulsion.	Active at the girth to maintain the impulsion.
Seat: More weight on the right seat bone.	More weight on the right seat bone.	More weight on the left seat bone.

IV

Indirect Rein
of Opposition
in front of
the Withers

V

Indirect Rein
of Opposition
behind the Withers
(Intermediate Rein)

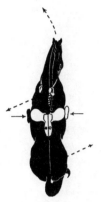 

Active, rotates at the wrist, fingernails facing up; acts slightly to the left in front of the withers.

Active, rotates at the wrist, fingernails facing up; acts slightly to the left behind the withers.

Passive, goes forward and down to yield, to allow, and then to regulate the action of the right hand.

Passive, goes forward and down to yield, to allow, and then to regulate the action of the right hand.

Active, at the girth to maintain the impulsion.

Active, behind the girth to push the haunches to the left.

Active, slightly behind the girth, stronger than the right, to encourage the haunches to go right when needed.

Active, at the girth, to maintain the impulsion.

More weight on the left seat bone.

More weight on the left seat bone.

About the Author

François Lemaire de Ruffieu grew up in France. He was first trained by Maître Jean Couillaud and graduated in 1967 from the Cadre Noir, one of the oldest and most prestigious riding academies in Europe. During his six years in the cavalry at Saumur and Fontainebleau, he studied and showed extensively in dressage, stadium jumping, three-day eventing, and steeplechase. He also taught riding in Paris at the Military School of War. Since coming to the United States in 1971, he has broken and trained yearlings, ridden as a jockey at several racetracks, and taught at numerous stables. In 1978 he started his own business and now spends most of his time giving clinics throughout the United States and Europe. His students have won year-end high-score awards in equitation, hunter classes, stadium jumping, dressage, and combined training. In 1987 he was appointed Executive President, France, for the Arabian Sport Horse Association (ASHA).